THE ROAD AHEAD

A.E RADLEY

HEARTSOME PUBLISHING

SIGN UP

Firstly, thank you for purchasing *The Road Ahead*.

I frequently hold flash sales, competitions, giveaways and lots more.

To find out more about these great deals you will need to sign up to my mailing list by clicking on the link below:

http://tiny.cc/theroadahead

I sincerely hope you will enjoy reading The Road Ahead.

If you do, I would greatly appreciate a short review on your favourite book website.

Reviews are crucial for any author, and even just a line or two can make a huge difference.

DEDICATION

For Emma.

CHAPTER 1

"Excuse me! Sorry!"

Rebecca rushed past an elderly couple. She looked at her watch and started to run towards the terminal building. Time was running out. She had to catch her flight, she couldn't afford to miss it. Around the corner, she almost collided with another elderly couple.

Apparently, the Algarve was full of them. Slowly meandering around, not caring if they were in the way. Usually appearing to be in a world of their own. They eyed her with confusion, probably wondering what the fuss was about. The concept of time seemed to be lost on most of them.

"Sorry!" she called over her shoulder as she sidestepped them and sprinted towards the airport entrance.

She knew she shouldn't have relied on the taxi service her hotel recommended. It seemed a little too much of a coincidence that the lazy receptionist shared a surname with the taxi driver. When he'd finally turned up, he seemed less interested in getting to the airport and more interested in his telephone call.

So much so that they missed the turn to the airport, adding to the delay.

The automatic doors parted, and she entered the building. She slowed her running to a jog, looking around in confusion. The departures terminal was packed with people standing around. Angry-looking people. Arms were folded, and a combined murmuring of displeasure filled the air. Something was definitely up.

Rebecca took a few steps forward and looked up at the ceiling monitors. Her eyes widened. Each and every flight on the departure board was marked as delayed.

"No, no, no," she whispered to herself.

A businessman was standing beside her, looking at his phone and shaking his head.

Rebecca turned towards him. "Excuse me, do you know what's happening?"

He looked up. "Some massive computer failure. Knocked out air traffic control in all of Portugal and Spain. Everything is grounded."

Rebecca swallowed. "Everything?" She removed her heavy backpack and lowered it to the floor.

He nodded. "Yeah, speak to a check-in assistant, but that's what they told me." He held up his phone for her to see the screen. "And that's what the news says."

"Did they say how long it would be?" Rebecca felt cold fear grip at her. She had to get home, she didn't have time for delays.

"No idea, could be ten minutes, could be ten hours. Personally, I don't think it will be that long. It can't be." He lowered his phone and gestured to the growing crowd. "This close to Christmas, they'll be calling everyone in to get it sorted out."

Rebecca looked around at the people in the departure hall.

In her mind, people and planes were like water and glasses. Water spilt from a glass always looked like so much more compared to water contained in one. It was the same with people. Sat on a plane, the number of people looked reasonable, but sprawled out in an airport, they seemed like enough to fill hundreds of flights.

She turned back to the businessman. He looked authoritative, some kind of higher-up executive, she assumed. In her experience, people like that didn't always have the best grasp on reality. They assumed that their personal assistant, faithful Marjorie, would fix everything in a jiffy. They didn't know that Marjorie had sold her kidneys, killed a man, and bribed law officials to do what needed to be done because she had a large mortgage, three children, and a beagle, and needed her job whatever the cost.

"Thanks," she said. She picked up her bag and made her way through the crowds to the check-in desks.

The long row of desks was manned by exhausted-looking staff who seemed to be struggling to maintain a customer-facing smile. Luckily, there were no queues. Most people had given up speaking to the airline staff and were now standing around looking discontent, delivering filthy looks to any staff member who made eye contact.

Hoping against hope, Rebecca walked towards a free desk.

"Hi, Rebecca Edwards," she introduced herself to the woman. She took her passport and her boarding pass from her pocket and handed them over. "I'm due to fly to Heathrow, but I hear there is a delay?"

"All flights are delayed at the moment. There is a computer problem and no flights can land or take off." The woman didn't even make a move to pick up her passport or boarding pass.

"Right," Rebecca said. She chewed her lip. "Any idea of time?"

"As soon as we hear anything, it will be announced over the speaker and on the screens." The woman pointed up towards the screens that hung from the ceiling.

"Okay…" Rebecca knew that there was nothing more to be done, but she couldn't bring herself to walk away from the desk. She lowered her heavy bag to the floor again, her mind racing as she wondered what to do next.

The illogical part of her felt that standing around the check-in desk would somehow help her predicament. The desk was a critical part in the whole boarding process. Somehow, being there gave her hope. But in her heart, she knew it was futile.

"I'm sorry, there really is nothing I can do." The check-in assistant offered an apologetic smile.

"I really need to get home," Rebecca said. She leaned on the high check-in desk, pushing aside a stand-up marketing message regarding the airline's award-winning customer service. "When do you think the next plane will leave?"

"I'm sorry, but I don't have any information to give you." The assistant, Beatriz if her nametag was to be believed, tapped some buttons on her keyboard while squinting at the screen.

"I know it's not your fault," Rebecca added.

She watched as an irate German woman yelled at the poor check-in assistant beside her. She'd never understand how someone could be so mean, especially to the people on the front line. Yes, the airport had a massive computer failure. Yes, planes were grounded. Yes, it was the twenty-third of December. But that was no reason to take it out on the minimum wage check-in assistants.

"Sorry about all the people shouting at you, it must really

suck," Rebecca said. She knew she didn't have to apologise for someone else's behaviour, but she wanted to.

The German woman left, blasting out obscenities as she went.

"It is a busy time of year," Beatriz replied. "Many people want to get home. The air traffic control systems have been down since early this morning, and we have no idea when they will be back up and running. It isn't just Faro Airport that's affected, it's many airports throughout the country. And in Spain, too."

"Must be horrible for you to have to deal with it," Rebecca sympathised. She fretted with her hair tie. She couldn't imagine having to tell hundreds of irate passengers that news, over and over again.

"In all my years of flying, I've never seen such incompetence!"

Rebecca winced at the British voice. She turned to look at who had taken over from the German woman to be in the running for rudest passenger of the morning.

The woman was approximately in her forties and wore a black skirt suit. Her long, blonde hair was perfectly styled in soft curls that fell to her shoulders. Rebecca glanced down at the woman's feet, noting a plaster cast on one foot, which looked at odds with the business attire. For a brief second, she wondered what had happened and felt a pang of sympathy towards her.

"I need to get back to London, now. How are you going to make that happen?" the woman demanded. She smacked her passport onto the check-in desk.

Rebecca's eyes widened at the tone. Her sympathy at the woman's cast evaporated. She turned back to Beatriz.

"Wow," she whispered and tilted her head towards the loud woman. "Rude."

Beatriz smiled and nodded in agreement.

"Don't know why she's complaining, she should fly her broom home," Rebecca muttered.

Beatriz chuckled. She looked thoughtfully at Rebecca for a moment. She leaned forward, gesturing for Rebecca to do the same.

Rebecca stood on her tiptoes and pivoted forward. She wondered why airport check-in desks were often so high. She was hardly short, but even she struggled to see over them sometimes.

"There were two planes to London due before yours," Beatriz explained, gesturing around the busy airport.

Rebecca turned around. She regarded the angry passengers standing around, most of them shaking their heads. The occasional tut could be heard.

"I can't say when the computer system will be up and running, but even if it sprang to life right now, the two planes from this morning would take priority. We don't have enough planes to take everyone today, and we can't divert from other airports as it's so close to Christmas."

Rebecca's heart rate picked up as she began to understand the reality of the situation.

"All of the other airlines will be fully booked," Beatriz concluded.

"You're telling me that my chance of getting home for Christmas is bad, right?" Rebecca guessed.

Beatriz nodded. "By plane, yes."

Rebecca frowned. "Is there another way? What about the trains?"

"Altogether impractical, miss. To travel from Faro to London, you would have to get to Lisbon, then take a night train to the Spanish-French border. Then, you'd have to switch to travel to Paris, and then switch again for the high-speed rail to London." The assistant frowned as if to emphasise her point. "A lot of transfers, and it could be expensive."

Rebecca's heart sank. "Not to mention the timing. I'd never get home for Christmas."

Something about her plight must have resonated with Beatriz. The woman gestured for Rebecca to come a little closer. She did the best she could, standing on the very tips of her Converse All-Stars. "Very soon, these people are going to realise that time is running out, and they are going to look for alternative methods of transport. You can, technically, drive to London and get home for Christmas. But there will be a limited number of cars available for hire…"

The penny dropped. Rebecca slowly nodded as she understood. Beatriz smiled, picked up Rebecca's passport and boarding pass, and handed them back to her.

"I'm sorry, Miss Edwards, there's nothing I can do," she said loudly.

"Thank you, thank you so much," Rebecca whispered as she grabbed the items and hoisted her rucksack onto her shoulder.

"You better hurry," Beatriz advised quietly.

"I will, thank you again," Rebecca said. She turned and looked at the airport signage, searching for a pictogram of a car and her way home.

CHAPTER 2

ARABELLA HENLEY awkwardly stalked the departure hall, leaning heavily on her crutch as she did. She couldn't believe the incompetence she was facing.

Air travel predated computers, and yet it was supposedly completely impossible to take off while the system remained down. No matter whom she spoke to, she couldn't get a proper answer on how long it would be until the situation was fixed.

She'd spoken to three separate customer service advisors, all of whom were completely useless. In the end, she had demanded to speak to a manager, and they'd sent her a four-teen-year-old boy. She chewed him out and then requested another manager. A grown-up emerged, only to mansplain that the computers were all down.

Of course, she already knew that the computers were all down. That was obvious. What she wanted to know was what they were going to do about it. And how, precisely, she was going to get back to London. Unsurprisingly, no one seemed to know the answer.

Eventually, she had grabbed her crutch and limped away from the check-in desks. If she'd stayed there a moment longer she would have been arrested by the Portuguese police for throttling a member of the staff.

As she left, she heard the assistant mumble something in Portuguese, presumably something not flattering. She decided to ignore it. She knew she was a difficult customer, maybe even rude. But that was how you got things done. That was how you ensured that people didn't walk all over you. Business was tough, life was tough, and so she was tough.

She stopped her circles of the departure hall. She leaned against a pillar and let out a sigh. The terminal building was busy. Extremely busy. It seemed that everyone wanted to get somewhere for Christmas.

"Do you know how long the computers have been down?" she asked a nearby couple. She knew they were British, she could tell by the pink skin and the dreadful clothes.

"Since this morning," the man replied. "We were supposed to take off at six o'clock."

She nodded and turned away, not wanting to encourage further conversation. She wanted information, not friendly chatter and new best friends for the next few hours. She looked at the clock on her phone, it was eight in the morning. The system had been down for at least two hours.

She glanced around the terminal building again. There were hundreds, probably even thousands, of people. All standing around, waiting for information.

She'd seen this before. When ice had closed Heathrow for a day, the results had been disastrous. A lack of planes, lack of runway take-off slots, and an abundance of people had led to severe delays. And that was a major London hub, more prepared to deal with large-scale problems than Faro on the Portuguese coast.

A middle-aged couple caught her eye. They were calmly piling their bags onto an airport trolley. Trying to look discreet, trying not to draw attention to themselves. Trying but failing. The look of panic in the man's eye gave him away.

What are you up to? she wondered.

The mother grabbed her escaping toddler by the wrist and pulled him towards the exit. The man was already hurriedly pushing the airport trolley that way, seemingly trying not to run.

Arabella watched them with interest, her gaze drifting up towards the airport signage.

"Of course," she mumbled to herself.

Rebecca felt faint. "I'm sorry, could you repeat that again?"

"Two thousand five hundred and fifty-eight euros."

She knew she couldn't afford it. Even so, she desperately tapped the amount into the conversion app on her mobile phone. It looked just as hideous in British pounds.

"It is one of the last vehicles we have."

She looked up and read his nametag. "Look, Jose, it's nearly Christmas and I have to get home. Surely you can help me out?"

Jose shook his head. "I'm sorry, there are many people in that terminal who would be willing to pay for that vehicle."

Rebecca heard the door to the car hire office open behind her. She turned to see a couple with a toddler hurry in and approach the desk next to her.

"We need to hire a car to drive back to England," the man explained to Jose's colleague.

Jose raised his eyebrow and looked at Rebecca. "See?"

Perhaps in the spirit of the holiday, this young family would like to car share back to the UK.

She tried to get the couple's attention, but they purposely busied themselves with their toddler and their phones to avoid eye contact. *Christmas spirit, my arse.* She was running out of options.

"Can I pay half now, half later?" Rebecca tried.

"No. Maybe try one of the other hire agencies?" Jose gestured towards the door with his pen.

"They're either closed or don't have any cars," Rebecca said. Inspiration struck her. "What about bikes? Do you have any bikes I can hire?"

Jose shook his head. "We don't hire out bikes."

He tapped on his keyboard and nodded towards the couple.

"We are now down to one vehicle. If you want to secure this vehicle, I would need to hold it for you now with a credit card. Can you afford it?"

"Maybe." She pulled her wallet out of the inside pocket of her leather jacket and grabbed two fifty-euro notes. She put them on the table. "Please, hold the car for me, I just need to make a phone call and get someone to transfer the money to my bank."

Jose looked at her sceptically. She couldn't blame him. The chance that anyone had the money to lend her was extremely slim, but he didn't know that. And she had to try.

He picked up the notes and put them under his keyboard.

"Ten minutes," he told her.

"Thank you, thank you." She scurried away from the desk,

sat in one of the waiting chairs, and pulled out her phone. She scrolled through her contact list, wondering who on earth she should call. Even if she did find someone who happened to have that kind of money rubbing a hole in their pocket a few days before Christmas, she had no idea how she'd pay them back.

She started to compose a text message that she could send to as many people as possible. She only had ten minutes. And that was if Jose kept his word.

She looked at the couple with the toddler. People from the airport were obviously starting to figure out that getting to wherever they were heading in time for Christmas was going to be difficult.

Rebecca knew that she needed to get in a car and begin the mammoth journey home soon. Not that she even knew how long it would take. She hadn't really stopped to consider the journey, the route, the time. She shivered. One problem at a time.

The automatic door opened. Rebecca looked up to see the rude woman with the cast limping into the hire office.

Shit, she thought and started bulk selecting her contacts.

Arabella entered the car hire reception. There were two people serving, one dealing with the couple with the toddler that Arabella had followed on the way over. The other had his back to her as he organised paperwork behind the desk.

Along the side wall some scruffy girl was texting. She presumed she wasn't in the queue, but even if she was, she wouldn't be for much longer.

She approached the desk and balanced her crutch against the side of it.

"I need a car, automatic, and I'll be driving it to England," Arabella said, drawing the attention of the man who was supposed to be serving.

"I'm afraid we don't have any automatic vehicles," he said as he turned to face her.

She rolled her eyes. "Fine. A manual will do."

He tapped on his keyboard. "That will be two thousand five hundred and fifty-eight euros."

Arabella chuckled and got her mobile phone out of her pocket. "You certainly know how to take advantage of a systems failure." She pulled her credit card from the mobile phone case and slid it across the counter.

"Hold on, Jose, you're holding that car for me!"

Arabella turned towards the scruffy girl and raised her eyebrow. "Apparently, he isn't."

"I'm sorry, but this lady has the means to pay immediately," he said. "You don't."

"I gave you a hundred euros!"

He picked up two fifty-euro notes from under his keyboard and held them out towards the girl.

The girl stood up and snatched the money back. "I can't believe this! You won't give me ten minutes to transfer some funds, but you'll give the car to someone with a broken leg."

He frowned and looked around the corner of the desk. He looked at Arabella's cast and winced. He pushed the credit card back across the counter.

"Sorry, I cannot let you have this car."

"What?" Arabella cried. "I can still drive, it's nothing. Just a minor... fracture."

"Fracture, broken," the girl mumbled.

"It would invalidate our insurance; my boss wouldn't allow me. This is a very expensive car," he explained.

"I'll buy more insurance. You can double the fee for hire, whatever you like, I need this car," Arabella told him firmly.

He shook his head and stood steadfast. "I'm sorry, I'm unable to lease any vehicle to you if you are not fully fit and able to drive it."

"I want to see your manager immediately," Arabella demanded.

"He's not here," Jose replied.

"This is unbelievable; how do you expect me to get home?"

He gestured towards the girl. "Maybe she could drive you? You are both going to England. She cannot afford a car, you can afford one but cannot hire one due to your leg. And it will be better for the environment to car share."

Arabella stared at him. The last sentence appeared to be his attempt at humour. An attempt that she didn't find particularly funny now. She looked at the girl. Being sat next to the girl for a two-hour *flight* would have been torturous, but driving all the way back to England with her?

"I'll do it," the girl said. "I have to get back to England. I'll drive all day and all night if you want."

Arabella looked from the girl to the assistant, wondering when they'd start laughing and admit it was all a practical joke. That moment seemed to be less and less likely the longer she watched them.

"Do you really think I'm just going to hop in a car with someone I don't even know? I don't even know her name." Arabella laughed derisively.

"Rebecca Edwards, that's my name. Look, we both want to

get home. He's right, we can either do this together or both be stuck here."

Arabella bit her lip and critically looked the girl up and down. She knew her options were limited, but she wasn't about to agree to jumping in a car with an unknown quantity until she knew it was her *only* option.

"And you have a full and clean driving licence?"

Rebecca nodded. "Never even had a parking ticket."

Arabella thought of her cast-iron mail rack at home with unpaid parking tickets overflowing. She was sure the speed camera in Kensington High Street had snagged her the last weekend. If it had, she may well be disqualified from driving.

"Where do you need to get to?" Arabella sighed as if the whole thing was a massive inconvenience to her personally. Which it felt like it was. So she wasn't a saint. But that was no reason for whatever higher beings might exist to be testing her so.

"Croydon. You?"

Arabella winced. Croydon was a dive. Of course it would be Croydon.

"Putney," she replied. It was some twisted kind of fate, their respective destinations were less than an hour away from each other. Geographically speaking. In terms of humanity, they were a million miles apart.

For a moment, Arabella was going to say no. It was her go-to reaction when she found herself trapped in a situation she didn't relish. Often, she'd even say no at her own cost, just because she could. Technically, she could say no. She could wait to see what the airport situation was, bully her way onto the first flight to London.

But then she ran the risk of being home late. Alastair and

her father wouldn't be happy about her missing the Christmas Eve party. She knew there was already an argument awaiting her when she got home, she didn't need to add to the situation.

The automatic doors slid open. She turned to see a man walk in, he had the gleam of desperation in his eye.

Decision made.

"We'll do it," she said. She held out her credit card for Jose. "Get us that car."

CHAPTER 3

"Oh my god, this car is brand new!" Rebecca squealed as they approached the vehicle. "A brand-new Mercedes. No wonder they wanted so much for it. I think we probably own a quarter of it by now. Well, you do."

Arabella massaged her temples. It was as if the girl had never seen a car before.

"More like a headrest," she corrected. "Now, our first stop is to return to the terminal building."

Rebecca looked over the car roof at her. "Why?"

"To get our luggage, obviously." Arabella opened the passenger door and regarded the seat. Getting in with her skirt and cast wasn't going to be pretty.

"I have my luggage," Rebecca said. She held up a tatty backpack for Arabella to see.

"That's your luggage? One bag?"

"Yep, hand luggage only. No extra fees and no chance it will get lost. Or accidentally flown to Azerbaijan."

Rebecca opened the driver's door. She reached into the car and pulled a lever and the boot slowly opened.

"Well, it doesn't change anything. We still need to go and get *my* luggage."

Rebecca placed her bag in the boot. "Don't tell me you just left your luggage in the airport? That's a security risk, you know. Someone's probably blown it up by now."

Arabella pinched the bridge of her nose. "I didn't just leave it lying around. I left it with the first-class lounge."

"There's a first-class lounge?" Rebecca closed the boot and walked to the driver's door.

"There's *always* a first-class lounge. Are we going to debate this forever or are we going to get going?" Arabella lowered herself into the car, careful to disguise the wince she felt bubble to the surface. The last thing she wanted to do was to show her new, no doubt troublesome, travel companion any weakness.

For all she knew the girl could be a murderer, preparing to mug her and then leave her on the side of the road somewhere. She'd already made a mental note to mention her kickboxing classes early in the journey.

Rebecca got into the car. "Do you want me to put your crutch in the back?"

"No." Arabella held onto the crutch. Which she now considered her improvised weapon, if needed.

Rebecca closed her door. "Fine," she mumbled. She put her seatbelt on and adjusted the mirrors. She started the engine and felt around for the seat controls.

Arabella narrowed her eyes as the girl moved a fraction of an inch back, and then forward. And then up, and then down. After a few minutes, she'd had enough.

"Are you enjoying yourself? Would you like to have a ride on the toy train inside the terminal?"

Rebecca continued adjusting the seat. "If I'm driving us all the way to England, I need to make sure I'm set up correctly."

"Of course. I'm just a little concerned that by the time you're perfectly comfortable, Christmas, and indeed New Year, will be a distant memory."

Rebecca ignored her and took her time adjusting the steering column before diverting her attention to the mirrors.

Finally, after what seemed like an eternity, she turned to Arabella.

"Right, I'm ready."

Arabella looked at her, wondering what the holdup was now. "Well? Do you want a round of applause? A medal?"

"Belt up."

"I beg your pardon?"

"Seat belt." Rebecca snapped her own seatbelt into place.

Arabella sighed. She reached around and grabbed her seatbelt and pulled it across her body, clicking it in place. "Happy now?" she asked.

"Oh, yeah, I'm ecstatic," Rebecca replied sarcastically.

Rebecca put the car into gear and then glided out of the parking space.

Arabella got her mobile phone out of her pocket and opened her navigation app. She wondered just how long she was going to be stuck with the snarky, potential murderer.

She clicked her home address and then requested directions from Faro Airport, Portugal. The app sprang into action, a revolving circle promising that it was thinking about the conundrum.

The map of the local area that she had been using grew

smaller as the map zoomed out to take in both locations. Suddenly, most of the Western side of Europe was visible. Portugal, Spain, France, and England filled her screen.

"Umm, do you wanna hop out?" Rebecca asked.

Arabella pulled the ticket receipt out from her inner jacket pocket and held it towards Rebecca without looking up from her phone.

"It would be quicker if you went, what with my leg. I'll mind the car."

A few seconds passed before Rebecca left the car, slamming the door behind her harder than was necessary for a new vehicle. She was clearly used to older cars. Arabella made a mental note to explain the features of modern cars to the girl once she'd retrieved the luggage.

But, for the moment, she was distracted. Looking at the map and wondering if she had put in the details incorrectly. It seemed ridiculous that the journey would take twenty-four solid hours. An entire day. She looked at the time and shook her head. She'd barely have enough time to have a shower and get to her hair appointment and massage before the party started.

She looked out of the window at the terminal building.

"Where is she?"

She looked at her watch and then sighed. This journey was going to be hell.

***

"Hi, I'm here to pick up luggage?" Rebecca asked as she approached the snooty-looking woman who manned the desk to the first-class lounge. The first-class lounge which had been impossible to find. Presumably hidden away from any old someone who might accidentally stumble into the luxurious surroundings and offend the proper clientele.

"Luggage for?"

Rebecca held up the luggage tag and looked at it. "Arabella Henley," she read. She then handed the tag to the sour-faced woman.

The woman looked at the luggage tag and then at Rebecca with uncertainty.

"She has a broken leg, she asked me to come to save her the journey." It was sort of true. She hadn't exactly asked. Arabella didn't seem to be the kind of person who asked favours. But Rebecca needed her, and so she'd put up with the rude behaviour. For now, at least.

"Oh, I remember." The woman nodded and picked up the telephone.

"Yeah, she leaves an impression," Rebecca muttered.

A quick conversation in Portuguese took place and then the phone was hung up. "It will be brought out in a moment. Wait here."

Rebecca tried to smile politely but knew she had probably only managed a constipated wince. The inference was clear. Wait here. Do not tarnish our first-class lounge with your presence.

She looked at her mobile phone for the first time since sending her message pleading for money. She scrolled through the replies. As she suspected, everyone was broke. They all wished they could help but ultimately couldn't. A few offered suggestions, none that were that useful.

Now she was stuck with some snobbish woman who was going to treat her like mud on her shoe until they got back to England. She still hadn't had a chance to discover just how long that journey would be, or even to plan a route. Part of her was in denial. She hoped that the whole situation was some terrible dream and that she was actually asleep on the Heathrow flight, whizzing her way back home.

"Miss Henley?" a male voice asked.

She looked up. "Close enough."

He gestured to a trolley beside him.

"You have *got* to be kidding me."

CHAPTER 4

"At last. Where have you been?" Arabella asked.

"Picking up Kim Kardashian's shoes," Rebecca gestured to the trolley laden down with five pieces of luggage in various sizes.

It seemed that first-class passengers still had to contend with wobbly trolley wheels. She'd struggled through the terminal, dropping a couple of pieces of luggage along the way and angrily shoving them back onto the stack.

"Who?"

She stopped by the car and stared at Arabella's confused face, where it was poking out of the open passenger window.

"Are you kidding me? You don't know who Kim Kardashian is?"

"Is it relevant to getting my luggage in the car and beginning this journey?"

Rebecca shook her head in dismay. This woman was going to be the death of her. She opened the boot of the car and moved her solitary rucksack out of the way. She started moving the bags from the trolley to the boot. She paused and moved some of the bags around. It was like an expensive Tetris puzzle.

"Do make sure—"

"If you tell me to be careful with your luggage, I swear I will throw it under the next bus," Rebecca shouted back.

She continued moving the heavy bags and cases around, eventually finding a way for most of them to fit. Her own bag would have to go on the back seat. Which would probably suit Arabella, who probably wouldn't want her luggage to be sitting handle to zip with Rebecca's aged rucksack.

She shouldered her rucksack and pushed the trolley back towards the terminal. She jogged back, slamming the boot and depositing her bag on the back seat. Then she hopped in the driver's seat. Finally, she could get out of this airport and get on with the journey home.

"We need to head for Seville, then north towards Bilbao, then into France, past Bordeaux, up to Calais, and across the Channel," Arabella informed her.

Rebecca reached for the engine start button with one hand, the other reaching for her seatbelt. "How long is that going to take?" she asked.

Arabella waved her hand. "Oh, you know these things, always overestimating. I'm sure if we get going we can knock around twenty percent off."

"How long does it say?" Rebecca asked again.

"I forget, twenty hours I think."

"Twenty hours?" Rebecca turned to stare at her.

"More like twenty-four with the time you wasted adjusting your damn chair."

"Shit, I didn't think it would be that long..." Rebecca

began to worry. She was meant to be hurrying home. She'd expected to be home by the afternoon, now that was impossible.

"It will just be longer the more we sit here," Arabella pointed out unhelpfully. "Seriously, I could just drive the car myself. I don't even know why I agreed to this farce."

Rebecca barked out a laugh. "Yeah, right, I see you wince every time you move your leg. You might be able to drive a little, but twenty-four solid hours of driving? You'd never make it."

"My leg is just fine, it's a fracture… nothing serious," Arabella defended.

"Right, if that's what you want to tell yourself." Rebecca reached into the back seat. She felt in the front pocket of her bag and pulled out her sunglasses.

Slipping them on her face she put her hands on the wheel. "Right, first stop, Spain."

Arabella leaned her head on the headrest and looked out at the countryside. It wasn't whizzing by. It was barely moving. Rebecca seemed to be one of those people who abided by every speed limit, even when the situation was dire. She checked the map again, wondering how much time she'd save if she could convince the girl to pick up the pace. She really didn't want to cancel her hair appointment at Carlucci's, but it looked horribly likely.

"You know, they're not as pedantic with speeding here as they are back home," Arabella offered.

"I'm not worried about being caught speeding."

"Oh, good. Well, you don't have to drive slowly for my benefit."

"I'm not. I'm driving the speed limit so we won't die in the event of a high-speed collision."

Arabella rubbed her temples. "If you drive properly then we won't have a high-speed collision."

Rebecca shook her head, not taking her eyes off the road. "I'm one factor. There's other drivers, weather conditions, road conditions. There's a reason why speed limits are set. It's to maximise our chances of survival if something goes wrong. I want to get home as much as you do, but I want to make sure I get there in one piece."

"I knew all of those advertisements regarding road safety were damaging our youth," Arabella said. "Fine, do continue to drive like a sloth."

"Thank you for your permission, I'll drive like a sloth. Who happens to be going seventy miles an hour."

Arabella rolled her eyes and continued to look out of the window. Her hair appointment was seriously in jeopardy. In fact, if Rebecca insisted on driving like a ninety-year-old, the whole Christmas Eve party could be in jeopardy. She wondered if she should call Alastair to let him know, or if that would just make him worry more.

At the moment, he was probably blissfully unaware of her predicament, assuming that his fiancée was about to board a flight home. She had a few more hours before she needed to tell him what had happened. She could be in France by then. Which sounded a lot better than being in Portugal.

Anything that delayed the conversation would be a bonus at this point. She knew Alastair would relish the opportunity to tell her again that she was wrong to go to Portugal. They'd argued about the point solidly for four days before she'd finally gone anyway.

"Spain!" Rebecca cried. "One country down."

Arabella looked at her watch. They had only been driving for forty-five minutes. It was a good sign, but it was just the tip of the iceberg.

"Just all of Spain, France, and the English Channel to go," Arabella muttered. "An hour and a half and then we'll be in Seville."

"Great, thanks so much for the encouragement," Rebecca replied sarcastically.

Arabella glanced at her, noticing her hands were tightening over the steering wheel. The girl confused her. She was in her late twenties, casually dressed, and with little regard for her appearance if her unkempt long, brown hair and her lack of makeup were anything to go by.

At first, Arabella had thought of her as a free spirit type of person, someone who drifts around with no real job and probably believes in the healing powers of crystals. And yet she fastidiously kept to the speed limit.

Now she looked frustrated, but she didn't elaborate on what was vexing her.

"What did I say?" Arabella asked.

Rebecca laughed. "You really don't know, do you?"

"Know what?" Arabella demanded.

Rebecca shook her head and focused on the road ahead, closing the topic of conversation with her silence.

Arabella leaned on the headrest again and looked out of the window. It was going to be a very long journey.

CHAPTER 5

REBECCA DIDN'T THINK she could take much more of Arabella's constant driving tips, directions, and updates as to how long the journey would take. They'd been in the car for under an hour, and already she wanted to put Arabella in the boot with her expensive luggage.

If Rebecca celebrated another milestone in their journey, Arabella was quick to point out how many more they had to overcome. The woman was impossible to please and it was making Rebecca stressed.

She looked at her hands, her knuckles white from clutching the steering wheel. She released her death grip a little and took a cleansing breath. She rolled her shoulders to relieve the tension. She wasn't going to allow Arabella to get to her. She didn't deserve that power over her.

I need to get to know her, humanise her a bit, Rebecca thought. *This is a weird situation. She's on edge. Once we break the ice, she'll be better. Hopefully.*

"So, what were you doing in Portugal, if you don't mind me

asking?" Rebecca asked politely.

"Completing the paperwork for the sale of a client's villa," Arabella said.

"Oh, cool."

"Not particularly. These countries always insist on paperwork being signed in person and cash in brown envelopes."

"Henley!" Rebecca suddenly clicked the pieces into place. "As in Henley's Estate Agents?"

"That's the one." Arabella sounded bored.

Henley's Estate Agents were well known in London. They had an office in every town, sometimes more than one. The offices were more than the average estate agent, they were beacons of modern design. Smooth angles, bright colours, faddish lights. Each branch was different, a piece of artwork in its own right. All were known for their luxurious comfort. Clients would be offered drinks from a range of fifty teas while they sat on leather sofas buying expensive properties.

Rebecca had never been in a Henley's. She'd never had the pay packet to be able to afford to step foot in one. She was sure an invisible scanner at the door would detect her financial status and a trap door would dispose of her before any of the staff members could be disturbed by her presence.

"I thought you only operated in London?" she asked.

"We have an international office, mainly Europe but some American properties, too. Mainly holiday homes. You know what it's like, after a few weeks exhausting yourself in London, you need a break in the sun."

"Absolutely," Rebecca replied. Of course, she thought the very idea was pretentious and unnecessary, but she was trying to make friends with the woman. She wasn't about to say that those kinds of riches were obscene. It wouldn't be right for her to say that she believed that vast wealth should be equally distributed and not held by the few. In their luxury holiday villas.

"You say you sold your client's villa?" Rebecca asked. "How will they take a break now?"

She didn't really care how Mr and Mrs Yah-Yah were going to rest themselves from the exhaustion of champagne galas and theatre opening nights. But it was the only topic of conversation she had open to her and she needed to bond with this woman somehow.

"They bought a yacht. They didn't want to be tied down to bricks and mortar."

"Of course." Rebecca shook her head slightly. This was going to be a tremendously long journey.

"I presume you were there working, too?" Arabella sniffed. "Some kind of bar work? Waitressing?"

Rebecca couldn't see Arabella, but she could feel the judgement radiating off her. The moment she met Arabella, she felt she knew everything she needed to know about her. But she'd given the snobbish woman the benefit of the doubt and tried to speak to her, to get to know her. Arabella apparently didn't do the same. She's taken one look at Rebecca and made up her mind.

It had been a short effort, but Rebecca had already had enough of being nice. It was clear that Arabella was judgemental, rude, and condescending. Everything Rebecca hated in a person.

"Yeah, bar work. And dancing, you know? Gotta make a living, right?" Rebecca lied.

"W-well, yes, I suppose so, yes," Arabella stuttered.

"And the tips are amazing, well, they are where I work, if

you know what I mean." Rebecca elbowed Arabella meaningfully.

"Eyes on the road," Arabella whispered, clearly uncomfortable with the conversation.

Serves you right, Rebecca thought.

She'd never tended bar in her life; she was one of those people who could only carry two drinks at a time, one in each hand. People who could carry three or more were like sorcerers. And as for dancing, two left feet.

But the comment had shut Arabella up for the meantime. Rebecca let out a breath and started to relax her grip on the steering wheel.

Arabella shifted uncomfortably in her seat. The Mercedes leather seats were sinfully comfortable but not when you had a cast, and not when you were embarking on a journey through four countries. Certainly not when you were trapped in the car with a prostitute.

She should have known. The long, brown hair, the thin, muscled body, and the ripped clothes. She knew rips were supposedly the fashion, but it just looked so messy to her.

She chanced a quick glance at Rebecca. They hadn't spoken for an hour. Not since Rebecca had told her about her employment and Arabella had been stunned into silence.

She'd briefly considered if she would survive opening the door and rolling to safety but decided to stick with her luggage. She was fairly sure her insurance wouldn't cover her for a duck and roll out of a moving vehicle.

She should have listened to Alastair and stayed home. She

should have sent someone else to complete the sale. It was just her pride and her feeling of losing control that made her see the job through to completion personally.

The wedding was three months away and already her workload was being distributed to others. Of course, she'd agreed to give up work once they were married, but she was surprised at the speed with which the date was arriving. Not that she could complain. Who wouldn't say no to a life of leisure?

Not that she currently felt she'd ever get to see that life. It was looking less and less likely that she would even make it home. Rebecca was probably going to kill her and leave her body somewhere in the Spanish countryside.

The girl was probably backpacking her way around Europe without a penny to her name. And now she was in a luxurious car with a named partner of one of London's most exclusive estate agencies.

Rebecca obviously knew that Arabella had money. She'd paid the exorbitant fee for the car hire, she had designer luggage, Rebecca had seen the credit cards in her wallet. She swallowed nervously. The girl knew a lot about her, and Arabella couldn't even remember her surname. She was certain the girl had said it at some point, but she'd instantly disregarded it as useless information.

She needed to get some information on the girl, something that would help the police to track her down in the event they ever managed to find Arabella's body in the scrubland.

"We should stop at the next station and get something to eat and drink," Arabella suggested.

"You sure you want to stop? That might add some precious minutes to our schedule," Rebecca replied.

"There's no point in arriving dehydrated."

"Fine. I'll stop at the next garage I see."

Arabella shifted nervously in her seat again. Rebecca didn't want to stop, presumably afraid that her face would be picked up on any CCTV present at the garage.

She wondered if she should contact Alastair. She didn't want her sister getting her hands on the Royal Doulton collection of ceramic coasters. Alastair wouldn't be aware of their value and would probably hand them over without thinking.

"You're in luck, there's a station," Rebecca said. She pointed towards the roadside sign promising that a petrol pump would be appearing in two kilometres.

She mumbled a reply and turned to look out of the window again.

Alastair would probably just tell her she was being silly. He always accused her of overreacting. Maybe sometimes she did overreact, but sometimes she was spot on. Of course, he only ever remembered the times she was wrong. She hated that he was right, that she shouldn't have gone to Portugal. Especially so close to the Christmas party. So she couldn't call him. She'd rather be murdered, knowing that her sister was finally going to get the precious coasters than listen to another round of 'I told you so'.

Rebecca started to indicate. Arabella looked at the upcoming garage with a sneer. Rundown would be putting it politely. Under normal circumstances, she'd never even consider slowing the car near such an establishment. Thank goodness she wasn't intending to go inside herself.

"Should I top up with fuel, so we don't have to stop again for a while?" Rebecca asked.

"Yes," Arabella answered. Anything to get Rebecca out of the vehicle for a while so she could do what she needed to do.

Rebecca pulled up beside a petrol pump. She reached into her jacket pocket and pulled out a tatty-looking wallet.

"I'll pay," Arabella said quickly. She handed over a handful of euro notes. Rebecca took them and placed her wallet on the centre console between them.

"Get me a water, and some kind of juice. No added sugar, though. If they have any fruit, that would be good too. But no pears, I hate Spanish pears."

"I doubt they'll do fruit in there," Rebecca said as she turned off the engine.

"Then get me some crackers, plain. No added salt."

"I really don't think they are going to have many healthy options, maybe you should come in and have a look—"

"No," Arabella said. "No, you go. You'll be quicker. My leg slows me down…"

"You seem nimble enough when you want to be," Rebecca pointed out.

Before Arabella could reply, Rebecca opened the car door and exited the vehicle. As the door slammed shut, Arabella let out a sigh. She watched as Rebecca examined the fuel cap and the petrol pump.

"Hurry up," she muttered.

She leaned back in her seat, listening to the sound of the fuel cap being unscrewed. A few seconds later she heard the rumbling of the old petrol pump and the whooshing of fuel entering the tank.

After what seemed like an age, she heard the click of the petrol flap being put back into place. She looked up and watched as Rebecca walked towards the garage.

As soon as she was out of sight, Arabella picked up the wallet from the centre console and opened it up. She slid the plastic cards out so she could look at them. There was a bank card and a credit card in the first compartment.

"Edwards, that was it, Rebecca Edwards," she whispered.

Next she saw a gym membership card and a library card. She looked up to check that Rebecca was still in the garage. Luckily the girl still seemed to be shopping.

Arabella turned her attention back to the wallet. There were a couple of photographs, one of Rebecca and an older woman and another of Rebecca and a younger woman. Arabella briefly wondered if they were previous victims but quickly pushed that thought aside as the older woman had a strong family resemblance, presumably her mother.

Then Arabella found what she was looking for, the driver's licence. She took the plastic card out of the wallet and snapped a couple of pictures of it with her phone. She noted that a Croydon address was printed on the licence. At least that part of the story appeared to be true.

Twenty-seven, she thought. *Practically a child.*

Her heart pounded in her chest. She quickly put everything back the way she found it and laid the wallet back on the centre console. She concentrated on controlling her breathing, trying to get herself under control before Rebecca returned.

At least now the balance of power felt a little more equal. She knew things about Rebecca. Okay, small things, like the fact that she was a member of a gym and a library. But she also had an address.

If she was going to be hacked to pieces and left by the side of the road, at least she'd know that Rebecca would be caught while lifting weights in a seedy Croydon gym. And probably given a substantial fine for overdue books at the same time. She looked the type.

CHAPTER 6

REBECCA WALKED BACK to the car slowly. She was enjoying stretching her legs and being out of the car, in the fresh air, away from Arabella.

She knew she had to try to keep the peace. Arabella certainly wasn't going to make any attempt. If they were going to get home without sitting in awkward silence for twenty-two hours, it was going to be down to her. As much as she didn't want to, she knew she'd need someone to talk to for the sake of her own sanity.

She opened the car door and got in.

"They had fruit, but you wouldn't have wanted it," Rebecca said before Arabella had a chance to open her mouth.

She closed the car door and started to take items out of the plastic carrier bag.

"Water, and a plain orange juice with no added sugar." She handed the items to Arabella. "In the absence of fruit, I got you some wholefood cold-pressed fruit and nut bars. That was the only thing that wasn't crisps or chocolate." She emphasized her point by pulling a packet of crisps and a small box of biscuits out of the bag.

Arabella took the juice and examined the bars.

Rebecca opened the box of biscuits and put the bag with the remaining items in the back footwell. She fished the notes and coins out of her pocket and handed them back to Arabella.

"What's this?"

"The change," Rebecca told her through a mouthful of chocolate and marshmallow. She picked up her wallet from the centre console and put it back into her jacket pocket. "I suppose you thought I'd keep the change?"

"No... not at all. I just... forgot."

"Mm." Rebecca wasn't taken in by Arabella's unconvincing tone.

"What... are you eating?" The posh woman was hiding something. She'd tried to change subjects but was now unable to mask her disgust at Rebecca's food choices.

Rebecca flashed her eyes in excitement. "Mallomars. They're a biscuit and marshmallow covered in chocolate. Only the best thing mankind ever invented. Want one?"

Arabella wrinkled her nose. "No, thank you."

She shrugged and pulled another two out of the bag. "Suit yourself." She then started the engine and pulled on her seatbelt. She checked her mirrors and started moving, eager to join the motorway again and get some of the long journey done.

A phone rang. Rebecca glanced to her side and watched as Arabella examined the screen and then cancelled the call. She didn't say anything, and the air was starting to thicken again. Rebecca knew it was up to her to try to lighten the mood.

"So, how did you get into the estate agency business?"

Rebecca asked, fishing for any topic of conversation that would stop them from sitting in silence.

"My father set up the company," Arabella replied curtly.

"And you wanted to join?"

Arabella shrugged. "It was never really mentioned. It was obvious that I'd go into the family business."

"Do you enjoy it?"

"I enjoy working."

Wow, she's hard work, Rebecca thought.

Arabella's phone rang again. She hurriedly cancelled the call.

"You can take that if you want," Rebecca offered.

"I know, you're not the reason I'm not answering."

Rebecca rolled her eyes at the tone. "Fine, I was just offering."

"It's my fiancé," Arabella admitted.

"Oh, he's probably worried about you." Rebecca wondered why she was cancelling the call. She seemed cold, but avoiding her fiancé seemed odd, even for her.

Arabella snorted a laugh. "Maybe. More likely that he is looking forward to gloating."

"Gloating? Why?"

"He didn't want me to come to Portugal, he wanted me to send someone else."

"Why?"

"You ask a lot of questions."

"Well, I don't have much else to do. We're going to be stuck together for a while, so we might as well talk about something."

Arabella remained silent for a few moments. "We're getting married, and he wants me to stop working. He wants me to wind down my work duties in preparation for that."

Rebecca blinked. "Wow, I have a billion questions."

"I don't expect you to understand; it's obvious that we live different lives."

Rebecca clenched her jaw. "I can still relate to other people. Just because I live my life doesn't mean I can't understand someone else's."

The phone rang again. Arabella let out a deep sigh. Rebecca thought for a moment that she was weighing up the best avenue available to her, continuing a conversation with her or speaking with her fiancé.

Finally, she opted for her fiancé.

"Hello, Alastair," Arabella answered neutrally.

Rebecca could hear the muffled sound of a male voice on the other end of the phone, but not clearly enough to make out any words.

"Yes, it's been… yes, well… I was…"

Rebecca tried to pretend she wasn't listening, but it was impossible. Arabella didn't seem to be able to get a word in. Normally she would have found it funny, someone putting Arabella in her place, but she almost felt sorry for the woman. She was supposed to be marrying this man. A man who she clearly didn't want to talk to. A man who now seemed to refuse to listen to her.

"I'm in a car, driving back. I'll be back in plenty of time," Arabella claimed. She paused. "Well, I don't know exactly where we are now. Close, I'm sure."

Rebecca looked at the screen on the dashboard and realised she could busy herself with setting the on-board satnav system. At least that way she wouldn't be fully focused on the awkward conversation happening beside her.

"We don't need to talk about that now," Arabella said in a softer tone. "There's someone here."

Rebecca tried to ignore the conversation, tried to focus just on programming the satnav and driving the car, but she couldn't help herself.

"I'm… car sharing. She's driving." Arabella leaned towards the passenger door. "Of course, yes. Just some girl. We'll be home soon."

Rebecca muted the volume on the satnav. The last thing she needed was a booming voice announcing that they would arrive at their destination in twenty-two hours' time.

"I know," Arabella whispered. She cleared her throat. "Yes, I will."

Rebecca almost felt sorry for her. Almost.

"I know. Well, there's not a lot I can do about it now."

Alastair's voice got louder, still indistinct, but he clearly wasn't happy.

"What's done is done." Arabella tried to lean further away from her. "It will be fine. I'll make sure of it."

Rebecca glanced at the screen as it calculated the journey to London. The map zoomed out and out. Eventually it showed the whole of France, Spain, and the bottom of England. If she hadn't been aware what she had taken on before, she was now.

"Now that isn't fair, you know that—Alastair? Alastair?" Arabella looked at the screen. She sat upright in her seat again and coughed delicately. "We… were disconnected."

"He was mad?" Rebecca asked, not wanting to acknowledge Arabella's obvious lie.

"A little," she confessed.

"Sounded like more than a little."

"He's very stressed with work at the moment," Arabella defended.

Rebecca laughed. "Wow, that old one, eh?"

Arabella glared at her. "What do you mean by that?"

"I mean that he was shouting at you and made you feel bad and you just defended him by saying he's having a hard time at work. That's no excuse. Did he even ask if you're okay?"

Arabella opened her mouth to reply but closed it again. She looked down at her phone.

Rebecca chuckled. "I'll take that as a no."

"I already know that he's worried about me, he just doesn't show it in that way."

"In what way?"

"Verbally."

"Wow. He can't even ask if you're okay. And you're marrying him?"

Arabella turned to her. "Yes, I am. And I'm lucky to have him, you don't know anything about him. Anything about us. Who are you to judge?"

"Me? I'm a nobody." Rebecca shrugged her shoulders. "I just think that the person you choose to spend the rest of your life with should treat you well. You shouldn't be avoiding their calls. You should want to talk to them, lean on them, know that they have your back."

Arabella didn't reply. Rebecca knew she had her ear, so she carried on. "Your partner should listen to you, not talk over you. You should be a team. With mutual respect."

Arabella laughed bitterly. "Nice dream world you live in."

"It's not a dream world," Rebecca defended.

"So, you're like that with your boyfriend? I didn't hear you having a beautiful, mutually respectful conversation with him."

"That's because I'm single and a lesbian. But," Rebecca added quickly before Arabella could say anything, "I have been in relationships like that. In fact, all of my relationships have been like that."

"Oh, you're—"

"Gay, yes," Rebecca said. She didn't mind coming out to people. And what was Arabella going to do if she didn't like it? Throw herself out of the car?

"Alastair isn't that bad," Arabella said, apparently ignoring Rebecca's admission.

"Do you love him?"

"Of course. Why would I be marrying him otherwise?" Arabella laughed.

"Lots of people agree to get married without being in love." Rebecca shifted in her seat. "I just think he should have been nicer to you, that's all."

Arabella turned to look out of the window. Rebecca glanced at her a couple of times before returning her attention to the road.

Clearly the conversation was over.

CHAPTER 7

ARABELLA PUT her hand down the side of her seat and felt around for the controls. The throbbing in her leg was getting worse, and she needed to adjust her position. Ideally, she needed to walk around and stretch her leg out, but she wasn't about to admit that to Rebecca.

Especially as they had been sitting in silence for nearly three hours.

Arabella wanted to say something to explain and defend Alastair. But the more she thought about it, the more she realised that she couldn't. As much as she hated to admit it, Rebecca was right. Alastair didn't respect her. Deep down, she'd always known that, and it hadn't bothered her.

She'd always prided herself on knowing the value of her own self-worth. She was well-educated, from a good background, and great at her job. If she did say so herself.

Alastair was handsome, rich, and the right fit. Her father adored him. Everything seemed right. Of course, it wasn't a fairy-tale romance, she didn't think those kinds of relationships existed. They were just for Disney movies. Encouraging children to want to grow up and not scare them with the reality of what life was really like.

But Rebecca seemed to believe in them. She'd spoken of respect and being a team. Arabella knew that she didn't have either of those things in her relationship with Alastair.

She'd replayed the conversation with him over and over in her head. She'd deliberately put forward a strong and well-composed image in Rebecca's presence. An image that had crumbled the moment she spoke to Alastair.

She had felt embarrassed. She'd stumbled over words, struggled to say what she wanted to say. Then she had been unable to finish a sentence. The whole conversation had been a disaster.

Her fingers grazed over a set of buttons on the side of the chair. She pressed one and sighed in relief as the chair slid backwards. She then pressed a different button and the chair started to recline. The blood flowed to her leg, and she wiggled her toes.

"Are you okay?" Rebecca asked.

"Fine."

"Are you sure, we could—"

"I said I'm fine," Arabella snapped.

Rebecca slowly nodded. She gripped the wheel tighter and sat a little straighter.

That was when Arabella felt something she wasn't all that accustomed to.

Guilt.

The girl was just being kind after all.

From her reclined position, she took the opportunity to properly examine Rebecca. The odds of her being a murderer or a thief had dropped substantially. Arabella knew not to trust anyone fully, but the girl did seem to be genuine. She'd shown more care and concern for Arabella in the last four hours than Alastair had in the last four months.

She knew that Alastair didn't wear his heart on his sleeve like Rebecca seemed to. They were just fundamentally different people. It wasn't like one was right and one was wrong.

But different people they were, and speaking to Rebecca as she would speak to Alastair wasn't appropriate.

"I'm sorry," Arabella said. "My leg twinges a little and it makes me snappish. I apologise."

"How did you break it?"

Arabella bristled at the memory. "I fell down some stairs."

"Ouch."

"Yes, marble stairs."

"Wow, sounds like you're lucky it wasn't worse."

Her mind flashed back to the evening in question. She'd been at a party at a hotel, losing track of time. Suddenly it was closing in on midnight and she realised she had to hurry to get home. A misstep had her falling down a flight of fifteen hard and unforgiving steps. The doctors at the A&E had said much the same thing her travelling companion did.

"Yes, I suppose I was lucky," she admitted.

"My ex broke her ankle," Rebecca said. "She was playing tennis, and she slipped and fell badly. Freak accident kind of thing."

"Sounds painful."

"Yeah, I had to look after her for two weeks. The doctor said she wasn't allowed to put her weight on it. So, I had to help her get dressed, get to the bathroom and stuff. Getting her drinks and snacks."

"Also sounds painful," Arabella commented with a wince.

The idea of having to care for someone else in that way made her skin crawl.

"No, it was fun," Rebecca assured.

"Fun? How on earth could it be fun?" Arabella genuinely wanted to know what kind of PR spin Rebecca was going to put on caring for an invalid.

Rebecca smiled. "We spent lots of time together, we watched movies, cuddled. I couldn't fix her, but I could take away some of the discomfort. You know when you're sick and someone brings you a drink or something to eat? When you have a cold and someone brings you some tomato soup just at the moment you need it?"

Arabella thought for a moment. She'd never had that. Then again, she'd never offered it to anyone else either.

"No, not really," she admitted.

"Even when you were a child?" Rebecca asked. She seemed surprised.

Arabella laughed. "Oh, especially not when I was a child. We were just left to get on with things."

"Wow, well... take it from someone who knows, it's nice to care for the people you love. It's nice to be that person, to make someone feel better. Even if you can't necessarily fix them. Not so they can reciprocate. Just for the sake of doing the right thing and being kind to others."

Arabella looked up at the girl in surprise. The bartending, possibly whoring murderer with an apparent heart of gold.

"Are you rolling your eyes at me?" Rebecca asked with a chuckle.

"Absolutely," Arabella joked. "Non-stop since you started talking. I'm concerned I'll get a migraine."

"Ha, ha." Rebecca shook her head, but a smile still graced her lips.

"You're a unique specimen, Rebecca Edwards," Arabella said.

"Thanks, I think." Rebecca laughed. "Seriously, though, if your leg is hurting then you should probably get out and walk a bit when we next stop. It's just going to get worse otherwise."

"Fine, next time we stop for fuel I'll do a couple of laps of the car."

Rebecca nodded her agreement.

Arabella sighed and moved her head from side to side. No matter how luxurious the surroundings, she didn't like long journeys. Now she was stuck in a car, not even halfway through Spain and already she was exhausted. There were miles to go. Over a thousand of them according to the satnav screen.

She glanced at Rebecca again.

For the first time, she wondered if Rebecca would have the stamina to drive them home without stopping. Of course, Arabella had told her that she must, and Rebecca had agreed. But could she actually do it? A whole day's worth of solid driving was a big ask. But the girl seemed determined.

Now she thought about it, she seemed *very* determined. Of course, the time of year brought that out in people.

"I assume you are driving home to spend Christmas with your family?" Arabella asked.

"My mum," Rebecca said.

"I see. And she lives in… Croydon, did you say?"

"Yeah. I promised I'd be home in time for Christmas. We spend every Christmas together no matter what."

Good, that means she's invested in getting home as quickly as I am.

"I'm sure she'll be very happy to see you," Arabella said.

"What about you? What are you doing for Christmas?"

"Well, there's a big party every Christmas Eve at my father's house. And then on the day itself it will be my father, sister, Alastair, and I. Some family members and business associates will come and visit us throughout the day."

"Of course. Peace and goodwill to all men and business associates," Rebecca said.

Arabella chuckled. "I know it's unusual to talk about business at Christmas, but we do. It's not all presents under the tree and homemade pies at my house."

"Sounds awful."

Arabella laughed. "You really speak your mind, don't you?"

"I don't mean to be rude, I'm just saying that, in my mind, Christmas is for family. You exchange gifts, eat treats, watch television. You just be together."

"Sounds awful," Arabella joked.

"You say that now, but you haven't tasted my homemade Christmas pies," Rebecca said.

CHAPTER 8

THE SUN WAS orange and hazy, low in the sky. They'd been driving for seven hours, and Rebecca was feeling a numbness creeping up her backside. Arabella had been adjusting her seat on and off for the past four hours, clearly trying to get comfortable. Now she was partially reclined. Sat so low that she was unable to look out of the window.

Rebecca had been watching the icon of their car on the satnav screen throughout the journey. It seemed to slowly crawl its way across Spain. Even now they seemed to only be two-thirds of the way across the country. She'd never really taken into consideration just how big Spain was before.

Apparently, it was easy to *say* that you were driving across two countries, but a different matter entirely to be *doing* it.

She knew that she needed a break. Even though she desperately didn't want to waste any time. She needed the bathroom, to walk around a little, and to stretch her back and legs out.

"I'm going to need to stop for a few minutes," Rebecca said.

She waited for Arabella's acerbic response.

"Good idea."

She glanced at Arabella in surprise. The older woman pressed the button on the side of her chair. The motor started to whir. She slowly rose.

"You look like a terrible Bond villain," Rebecca commented.

After another thirty seconds, Arabella finally arrived at an upright position. "Where's the next services?"

"We seem to be in the middle of nowhere. I've not seen any services as such, the odd petrol station that looks rundown but nothing else."

"Well, that can't be as bad as the place we stopped before."

Rebecca snorted. "The places we've been driving past make that look like a palace. We're really out in the sticks."

Arabella got her phone out and started to tap away on the screen. "There must be somewhere around here where we won't catch tetanus."

Rebecca looked around the road. For as far as she could see in all directions, there was nothing. Scrubland and the odd wreck of a building. Closed hotels and bars were few and far between.

"We're in the middle of nowhere," Arabella announced.

"I told you." Rebecca smothered a yawn behind her hand.

"What was that?" Arabella asked.

Rebecca frowned. "Nothing."

"That wasn't nothing, you yawned."

"It was just a small yawn, nothing much. I'd drink more of my energy drink, but I don't want to do that until I know we're near a bathroom."

Arabella looked up at the scenery. "Maybe we should pull off the road? Look for a town?" She looked back at her phone and started to tap in a new search.

"There's a garage about forty minutes up the road we're on," Arabella said. "It's a dive, but it promises to have a bathroom, petrol, and food. Or we can turn off and be at a garage in twenty minutes, but we will be heading generally away from our route."

Rebecca pressed lightly on the accelerator pedal, pushing the car ever so slightly over the speed limit. It wasn't something she was comfortable doing, but she wasn't about to start going backwards.

"I can hold on for forty minutes, you?"

"As long as you're sure?" Arabella asked. "I mean, I don't want you to kill us both."

Rebecca rolled her eyes. "You nearly said something nice then."

"I've said plenty of nice things," Arabella defended.

"Must have missed them." Rebecca winced at her own tone.

She didn't want to speak to Arabella like that, it wasn't in her nature to be rude. She was just getting frustrated with the situation. She desperately wanted to be home and her back was aching, but that was no reason to take it out on a *nearly* innocent bystander.

"Then you'll just have to pay more attention, I'm not likely to repeat them," Arabella said with a jokey tone.

Rebecca smiled. It would have been easy for Arabella to reply sarcastically, but she hadn't.

Maybe she's not that bad, Rebecca thought. *Just takes a while to get through the thick skin.*

"I'll listen out for them," she promised.

"On reflection, I'm not sure I want that walk around the car after all," Arabella said as they pulled into the garage and came to a stop.

Rebecca leaned forward and wrapped her arms around the top of the steering wheel. She looked at the rickety old shack. The building looked like it was made of scraps of wood and metal and was precariously close to the edge of a steep cliff.

There were no petrol pumps, just tyre tracks that had burrowed a groove into the ground in front of the building. A cardboard sign, written in marker pen, hung clumsily by a single nail on the door. The light of the setting sun made it all the more ominous.

"How's your Spanish?" Rebecca asked, indicating the sign.

"Ring for service," Arabella translated.

Rebecca looked at the old-fashioned brass bell that hung by the door. "Right, so I should—"

Arabella grabbed her forearm and spun to face her. "Do we want to do this? This is the kind of place where innocent travellers like you and I go missing."

Rebecca scoffed. "Says who?"

"Movies!"

"Yeah, on a Halloween fright night special, maybe. The last movie I saw was a musical. No one died. In fact, everyone was happy and dancing."

"Why am I not surprised?"

Rebecca shook her head and removed Arabella's hand from her arm. "I'm going to ring the bell. If an axe murderer appears, beep the horn to warn me, okay?"

She opened the door and got out of the car. Stretching her hands above her head, she enjoyed the sounds of her lower back cracking. She walked towards the shack, examining the property for any signs of life as she went.

An old caravan was parked around the side of the building, but she couldn't tell if it was lived in or abandoned.

A thought occurred to her that the whole place might be abandoned. They may have driven forty minutes to find a closed garage. Maybe the next one was an hour away. She was pretty sure her bladder wouldn't survive that kind of wait.

She reached up and rang the bell a couple of times, hard.

She took a step back and looked around for any attendants. She looked at Arabella, who had shrunk back into her seat and was anxiously looking around.

Suddenly the door opened.

"Si?"

Rebecca spun around to address the elderly man standing there. "Oh, hi, do you speak English?"

The man looked from her to the car. He was a frail, tiny thing. "Gas?"

"Yes." Rebecca nodded her head. "And, a bathroom? Toilet?"

The man looked at her with a frown.

"Lavatory?" Rebecca tried.

He smiled and nodded in understanding. He indicated around the building, the opposite side to the caravan, towards the cliff. Rebecca wondered if he was suggesting she find a bush.

"Thank you," she said. "Um, I mean *gracias*!"

She turned to see Arabella struggling to get out of the car.

"Jesus," she mumbled under her breath. "Why doesn't she ask for help?"

The man disappeared back into the shack, and Rebecca walked over to the car to assist Arabella.

"You okay?"

"What did he say?" Arabella asked, pulling her crutch from the car and leaning awkwardly on it.

"He said 'gas'," Rebecca said. "And I said yes."

"Is there a bathroom?"

"Apparently around the corner." Rebecca gestured with her thumb. "Are you okay?"

Arabella struggled to stand straight, leaning heavily on the crutch. "Yes, just a little stiff."

"Same here."

She heard a noise and turned around to see the Spanish man exiting the shack with a large petrol canister that was half the size of him. He walked over to them.

"*Hola, hola,*" he greeted Arabella. He looked at the car and made an unlocking gesture towards it before looking at Rebecca.

"Oh, right, yes… *sí,*" she said. She walked around the car, leaned in through the driver's door, and unlocked the petrol flap.

The man immediately opened the flap and started to undo the cap.

"I'm going to the bathroom," Rebecca announced.

"Don't leave me here," Arabella whispered through clench teeth.

"You're welcome to come, but no listening."

"How crass," Arabella muttered.

She struggled to pivot herself. Rebecca moved to stand beside her and easily slipped her arm around Arabella's waist.

"Lean on me," she instructed. "You need to get blood flow back into your leg."

Arabella slightly leaned on her but seemed insistent on doing the majority of the work herself.

They started to walk away from the car, Arabella occasionally turning to look at the man.

"What if he steals the car?"

Rebecca turned and looked at the car. She gestured to the shack. "Then you get the caravan and I get the garage."

"I'm telling you," Arabella said. "This is where we're going to die."

"Do you always overreact this much? I'm surprised you even got in a car with me. What if I was a murderer?"

Arabella was silent, only the sound of the dusty ground under her crutch and plaster cast was audible.

"Oh my god, you thought I was a murderer, didn't you?" Rebecca laughed.

"I was cautiously concerned about you; I didn't know who you were," Arabella defended. "I mean, look at you."

Rebecca shook her head and laughed some more, ignoring the comment about her appearance. "So, the natural assumption was that I was a murderer?"

"I'm not sure what's so funny," Arabella said. She pulled away from Rebecca and started to walk on her own.

They approached the side of the building. A narrow path near the cliff edge led to a wooden outhouse that had seen better days.

Arabella stopped walking and turned up her nose at the rundown structure.

"I suddenly don't hear nature calling so loudly," she said.

"Tough, we're not stopping again until we get to, like, France. I'll go first," Rebecca said.

"Oh, yes, you do that. I'll just wait out here with the murderer," Arabella called after her. "Well, the new murderer, I suppose."

Rebecca smiled to herself and walked towards the wooden outhouse. She had to admit, Arabella wasn't quite the worst travel companion in the world. Now and then, she could actually be quite funny. Unfortunately, those bouts of humour were sprinkled in between judgemental comments.

She opened the door to the outhouse and peeked inside, holding her breath as she did. She looked around, pleasantly surprised at what she found. A clean, modern toilet. A sink. Soap. It was luxury compared to what the exterior of the building had promised.

She attended to her needs and then left the outhouse, ready to tell Arabella about the five-star facilities she'd discovered. Looking up the path, she couldn't see Arabella anywhere. She frowned and started to take a step forward.

"Rebecca, look at this."

She turned and looked at the back of the shack. "Arabella?"

"Around here, look at this."

She walked around the back of the garage and saw Arabella standing on the edge of the cliff. Rebecca walked up beside her in awe. The raised position allowed for miles and miles of uninterrupted views. Mountains in the distance, animals grazing, the odd farmhouse. The view was unlike anything she'd seen before. And the way the evening light shone on the valley was casting beautiful shadows and shades of reds and oranges.

"Wow," Rebecca breathed.

"Isn't it amazing? We couldn't see this because of the angle of the road, but we appear to be quite high up."

"Wait right here," Rebecca instructed. She took off at a sprint, running around the building and back to the car. The attendant looked at her with a kind smile. She returned the smile and retrieved her backpack from the back of the car.

She opened the worn flap, removed a couple of items of clothing, and then pulled out her camera. She paused and regarded the lens for a moment before digging in her bag for her wider-angled lens.

The man looked at her and smiled. "Click, click," he said, gesturing to the camera and then to the building.

Rebecca nodded. "Sí!"

She sprinted back around the building. This was what she loved about travel, you never knew where you might come across the most amazing shot. The view had been completely hidden behind some rundown old buildings. Many people would have driven straight by without having any idea of the wonders that lay a few metres away.

Back at Arabella's side, she raised her camera, took a shot, and then looked at the screen, examining the lighting data. She made a couple of changes to the ISO settings and then tapped the shutter again. She meticulously framed the view, adjusting the lens focus by a fraction each time she took a new shot.

She was lost in her own world, taking distance shots, close-ups, and everything in between. She knew from experience that the chance of her fully documenting the view was unlikely. Photos could never live up to the actual experience. Sometimes, though, tiny details could only be picked up in post-production.

The light was fading. This meant she must rush to capture the scene, as it grew more beautiful with every passing moment. As the winter sun set, the colours became richer and cast dramatic shadows across the valley.

"Hello? Earth to Rebecca?"

She lowered her camera and looked at Arabella in confusion. "I'm sorry?"

"I've been talking to you, but you've been in your own little world," Arabella grumbled.

"Sorry, I… I didn't hear you. What did you say?"

"I was commenting that your camera looks very expensive. Professional, even."

Rebecca looked down at her kit. "Oh, yes, it is."

"I thought you worked in a bar?"

Rebecca smirked. "Yes, you did. I might have misled you."

Arabella raised an eyebrow. "You don't work in a bar?"

Rebecca shook her head.

"You let me believe—"

"No, you assumed that because I don't look like you, I must have some low-paid, temporary job. So… I didn't give you information otherwise." Rebecca lifted her camera and took another shot. The sun was setting over a mountain and the light it cast was too beautiful to miss. "I'm a professional photographer. I was in Portugal doing a shoot for a band. Fun work but doesn't pay much."

"You're a photographer?" Arabella repeated, clearly taking a while to catch up with events.

Rebecca lowered the camera. "Yup. Not a stripper, or whatever you thought I was when you totally judged me by my appearance."

Arabella's mouth curled into a grin. "Well, you got me. I apologise for my assumptions about you."

Rebecca couldn't help herself, something about Arabella's stance, her smile, the way the wind blew gently through her hair. She raised her camera, wanting to capture the moment. She snapped a couple of pictures before Arabella began to laugh and bat the attention away with her hand.

"Oh, don't, I'm terribly unphotogenic."

"Are you kidding me?" Rebecca cried. "You're beautiful."

Arabella laughed and looked down at the canyon floor, obviously embarrassed by the attention.

Rebecca lowered her camera. "I'm sorry, I'll stop." She smiled.

"Good." She adjusted her hand on her crutch. "I'm going to use the bathroom. I assume it wasn't too horrible, as you survived?"

"You'll be pleasantly surprised," Rebecca reassured her.

"Good. You can continue taking your pictures, but no more of me." Arabella started to walk away. "I know where that can lead, I saw *Carol*," she joked over her shoulder.

Rebecca burst out laughing. "I thought you only watched slasher flicks."

Arabella paused and turned around. "It was practically a thriller. I was on the edge of my seat the entire time. They were lesbians, I was terrified they'd be killed."

She turned and started walking towards the outhouse again. "Thank goodness for a happy ending," she called back.

CHAPTER 9

ARABELLA LOOKED at the time on her phone. It was seven in the evening. They'd been driving for ten hours and were about to enter France.

At the outset, the journey had seemed doable. Now, not even halfway in, it seemed ridiculous to think they could drive back to England in one sitting.

Despite stopping and admiring the amazing view at the petrol stop a few hours ago, she was again feeling the pain of sitting still. Her leg was numb, as was her back and her backside. But worse than that, she could feel herself drifting off to sleep. The mind-numbing country views had given away to nothing but darkness. As soon as the sun had set, she'd longed for an abandoned farmhouse or scrubland as far as the eye could see.

Her efforts to engage Rebecca in conversation had been futile. It seemed that the girl didn't want to speak about herself or her personal life. And the more she retreated into her shell, the more Arabella tried to prise her out of it. With no success.

She now knew that Rebecca was not a bartender, a dancer, nor a prostitute. She was a photographer. Who lived in Croydon and wanted to get home to spend Christmas with her mother. Other than that, she was a mystery. Oh, and she was gay.

Arabella didn't even know why she wanted to know more about Rebecca. At first, she had wanted to learn more about her potential murderer. To somehow make a connection between them so Rebecca would be less likely to mug her and leave her for dead in an abandoned farmhouse.

But that wasn't the case anymore. Now she trusted Rebecca. As much as she trusted anyone, anyway.

She looked at the road and spied a promising sign up ahead.

"France," she said. She turned to Rebecca and smiled.

Rebecca didn't return the smile. She sat forward, focusing rigidly on the road. She looked exhausted.

"Another country down," Arabella tried again.

"Yup," Rebecca bit out.

They hadn't known each other for long, but Rebecca's silence was worrying. Arabella returned her attention to the road. They were passing over a bridge, with the promise of a toll booth up ahead. She looked at the satnav and saw that they had another thirteen hours to go. They weren't even halfway home. Rebecca looked utterly exhausted.

"Maybe we should stop?" Arabella suggested carefully.

"Ha! You're the one going on about how long this is taking and how late you'll be for your party. No, we keep going."

Arabella frowned at the outburst and turned to look out of her window.

"I'm sorry," Rebecca said. "I'm just a little tired, I didn't mean to snap at you. I'll get my second wind soon."

"It's okay, it's a lot to take on," Arabella said. "I do think we should stop."

"What time does your party start?"

Arabella looked at Rebecca. She knew what she was thinking. She wanted to work backwards from the start of the party and tell Arabella that they didn't have time to stop. Suddenly she felt an uncomfortable guilt for having pressured Rebecca so much at the start of the journey.

"Well, it starts at nine," she lied. "But it goes on until Christmas morning. I don't have to be there at nine."

"What about your hair appointment? You said that it was imperative that you made that appointment. And your massage, let's not forget your massage," Rebecca mimicked Arabella's tone.

She let out a sigh. "I may have said that in order to encourage you to drive a little faster. At this point I'll just settle for turning up to any of the party. You know, alive. And not wrapped around some tree in France because you crashed due to exhaustion."

"I'm fine," Rebecca argued.

The car slowed to the toll booth, and Rebecca pressed the button to open her window. They'd been through countless tolls in Spain, Arabella complaining at the ridiculous cost of each one. She thought they were all a scam, the country extracting money out of road users with no alternative.

The automatic booth flashed up an amount. Rebecca picked up a large handful of coins that she had stored in the cup holder. She looked at the coins with a frown on her face. Something she'd not done before.

It suddenly became obvious that Rebecca was struggling to identify the denominations of the foreign currency. Something that hadn't happened before and was clearly another sign of her tiredness.

Arabella waited a few moments before picking the correct coins out of Rebecca's cupped hand and holding them for her to take.

Rebecca took the exact change and threw it into the automatic change counter. A few seconds later the barrier opened.

"I'm fine," she repeated.

"Okay," Arabella replied.

Of course, she knew that Rebecca wasn't fine. They needed to stop, and a ten-minute break at a petrol station in the middle of nowhere wasn't going to cut it. They needed to stop for the night.

She wasn't even the one driving, and she was finding it almost impossible to keep her eyes open. They couldn't go on, even if Rebecca seemed adamant to do so. Arabella couldn't believe that she was just doing it so she'd get home in time for the party.

She assumed there was another reason for Rebecca's desire to get home as soon as possible. Probably to watch some inane television program, some overly advertised Christmas special perhaps. Or to participate in some tradition that her family upheld every year, eating a mince pie, or unwrapping one present before sitting in front of the television in a drunken stupor and a onesie.

Well, that wasn't going to happen if they carried on the way they were. They had to stop and rest for the night. And she had to make it happen.

She unlocked her phone and opened her accommodation application. She hoped that it wouldn't be too difficult to find somewhere to stay so close to Christmas.

"What are you doing?" Rebecca asked.

"Playing Angry Birds," she lied.

"I don't see you as an Angry Birds kind of person."

"Oh, I love it." She tapped in her requirements for the search filter. "Those birds. Being... angry."

"Yeah, I can tell you're a real fan."

"Why don't you talk about yourself?" Arabella changed the subject.

"What do you mean? I talk about myself."

"Not really. You lied about your profession, supposedly to teach me a lesson about making assumptions. Aside from that, you've evaded many of my questions."

Rebecca chuckled. "I've not *evaded* your questions."

The spinning search icon appeared while her phone sought out a connection. "If you say so."

"Ask me something, something I've supposedly evaded."

"There's nothing specific, just that you don't say anything."

"Maybe there's nothing to say? Maybe I'm just boring?"

"You've flown to Portugal to photograph a band, that doesn't sound *too* boring."

"Thanks, I think. And that was just one job. Their original photographer dropped out at last minute and they asked me to do it."

"You don't sound like you wanted to do it?" Arabella asked. She thumbed through a few hotels, checking for available rooms and a green light to indicate that the owner was online. No point in booking a last-minute room and surprising the host by turning up ten minutes later.

"I didn't. Didn't really want to be away from home, you know?"

Arabella laughed. "Not really. I wanted to be away from home."

"How come?"

Arabella paused as she thought about her reply.

She knew the answer, she just wasn't ready to verbalise it yet. Luckily, she was saved from the awkward truth by the search result providing its response.

"Take the next left."

"What? Why?"

Arabella sighed. "Just do it."

She was thankful that she had all her details saved on the application so she could take advantage of one-click booking. She felt the car starting to slow down and knew that Rebecca was doing as she had asked.

"What are we doing?" Rebecca sounded frustrated.

"Continue up this road for a kilometre and then turn right." Arabella quickly went back into her search result to secure another bedroom. While she didn't think Rebecca was a murderer, she wasn't about to share a room with the girl either.

"Arabella?" Rebecca asked, anger creeping into her voice.

She secured the second room and lowered the phone.

She turned to Rebecca.

"We're stopping. I've booked us in at a local bed and break-fast. No arguments. There's no way you can carry on like this. We'll stop for the night and get started early in the morning. By my calculations, we should get into London around seven in the evening on Christmas Eve."

"No, I told you, I'm okay to carry on, I—"

Arabella leaned over and put her hand on Rebecca's knee. "You're unable to keep your eyes open, you're smothering yawns, you've drifted lanes seven times in the last hour and that is only going to get worse. I know you're desperate to get home. But Christmas will wait a few hours longer. You're exhausted, and you need to rest."

She removed her hand and leaned back, waiting to see if Rebecca would argue the point or give in and accept that it was time to rest.

"You know, if this is an excuse to seduce me, forget it. You're not my type," Rebecca joked.

Arabella laughed. "Damn, you got me," she replied.

Rebecca sighed, seemingly resigned to the fact that they would have to stop. "Okay, so where is this bed and breakfast?"

Arabella breathed a sigh of relief. She picked up her phone and accessed the map. "It's about ten minutes away. It seems to be in the middle of nowhere, but then a lot around here seems to be in the middle of nowhere. Luckily for us that means it has two rooms available at short notice."

"But we start again early in the morning, right?" Rebecca pressed.

"Absolutely, I'm used to an early start, so whatever time you want to set off is fine by me."

Rebecca nodded. She slowed down and started to indicate right. "This road?"

Arabella looked at the map on her phone and then at the fog-covered road. The further they moved from the main road, the thicker the fog seemed to become.

"Yes, seems to be the one."

The road was narrow and set between two tall stone walls. The farther they went, the thicker the fog seemed to get.

"I can hardly see," Rebecca said.

"Just go slowly," Arabella said calmly.

She didn't feel calm. The fog was so thick that she could

barely see the end of the bonnet. If another car came from the other direction they would be stuck. There was no room to pass with the stone walls on either side of them.

Arabella held her breath as Rebecca slowly navigated the road. She saw an email come in from the bed and breakfast owner, confirming their bookings and advising them that they were expecting their arrival. She quickly typed a response back to say that they were in the area and would arrive momentarily.

She looked up again and swallowed. The road was so narrow and the fog so thick. If she'd known this was the road in, she would have chosen somewhere else. On the bright side, the adrenaline rush was sure to wake Rebecca up for a while.

After a few heart-stopping moments, the walls ended, and the road expanded to two lanes again.

"Where now?" Rebecca asked.

"It should be up here on the right," Arabella replied after checking the map on her phone.

Rebecca slowly drove, leaning forward and looking out of the window to the right.

"Are you sure? I mean, if you wanted to kill me and leave me out here—"

"Don't be silly," Arabella said. "It's here. Somewhere."

She looked at the phone again and then at the GPS map on the car dashboard.

"It should be a few more metres," she said.

A brick wall started to emerge through the fog. As they continued to crawl forward, the wall gave way to a large, open wrought-iron gate.

"Whoa." Rebecca stopped the car and looked at Arabella. "Bed and breakfast? Are you kidding me?"

Arabella looked at the mansion beyond the open gate,

shrouded in wispy fog. A pebbled driveway led to a set of stone steps which in turn led to an imposing front door. Two large lanterns illuminated the door. It was very gothic, presumably very grand-looking in good weather. However, in the fog it just looked eerie.

"It said Château de Bernard, but everything is a Château around here," Arabella argued. She looked at her phone and then at the building again. "This must be it."

"What if it isn't?" Rebecca asked.

"Then we apologise and drive out again." Arabella pointed towards the gate. "Come on, let's go."

CHAPTER 10

"You know, I'm suddenly feeling wide awake," Rebecca said. "Maybe we should, you know, keep going?"

Arabella glared at her.

"Okay, I'm going, I'm going." Rebecca took Arabella's phone, the booking receipt open and visible on the screen. She opened the car door and got out.

She swallowed hard as she looked up at the imposing building. It looked like something out of a crime drama. This was where Countess McDeath lived, appealing to the police that she was feeding her horses at the time of the murder, the tiny fact that she was feeding the horses body parts of the victim only coming to light at the end of the show.

Arabella rapped on the window, and Rebecca jumped. She turned and stared at her. Arabella waved her away from the car and pointed towards the front door.

"Wish I was the one with the broken leg," Rebecca muttered.

She turned back towards the house. The house that was

surrounded by an eerie fog. Why couldn't Arabella have picked somewhere a little less creepy? A generic chain would have been just fine. Not that she suspected many of them were available in the French countryside.

The wind started to pick up, and she wrapped her leather jacket around her body, only now realising that she was driving north in winter. It was going to get a lot colder. Although not as cold as she felt now, the atmosphere chilling her more than the weather ever could.

She took a steadying breath and made quick work of the front steps. Before she had time to reconsider, she pulled on the large metal hoop to ring the bell. She'd not seen an old-fashioned doorbell in person before, but she'd watched enough period dramas to know what it was.

She heard a dim chime sound inside the house. As tired and exhausted as she was, she hoped that the house was empty. Everything gave her the creeps about the building. She wanted to be back in the car and making her way home.

The sound of footsteps became audible. She took a tiny step back and glanced towards Arabella in the car. She knew that if anything happened, the older woman would be out of the car and charging an assailant with her crutch in a matter of moments. She was struck by the thought that Arabella, an unknown quantity half a day ago, was now her security blanket.

The door swung open.

"Miss Henley, I'm assuming?"

An elderly British lady stood in the doorway. She was tall and extremely thin. She wore a tartan skirt suit, and her hair was swept up into a bun. She looked like the kind of person who had never worn a pair of jeans, but she was smiling and seemed friendly enough.

"I'm Rebecca, Rebecca Edwards. Miss Henley's in the car. We were just checking we have the right place," Rebecca replied.

"Indeed, you do. I'm Mary Davenport, and this is Château de Bernard. Shall I ask my husband to help with the bags?"

Rebecca shook her head, she didn't think Arabella would want some unknown person touching her luggage. Nor did she want to ask an old man to drag Arabella's seventy-two cases up the stone steps.

"No, thank you. We're not sure what we're bringing in and what we're leaving in the car."

"Not a problem, I was just getting some tea ready. Would you both like some tea? Maybe some sandwiches?"

Rebecca felt her heart soar at the thought of a hot cup of tea. "Yes, please, that would be amazing."

Mary nodded and stepped back into the house, leaving the door open.

Rebecca hurried down the stairs and opened the car door. Arabella was literally on the edge of her seat, hands wrapped around her crutch.

"This is the right place," Rebecca confirmed.

Arabella let out a relieved sigh. "Ah, yes, well, I did know that. Of course it is."

Rebecca rolled her eyes. "Yep, of course you did. Anyway, we need to get our luggage in. And by our luggage, I mean yours. What bag do you want? Notice I said bag, singular."

Arabella balked. "I need at least three!"

"No, you don't. You're infirm, and I'm not dragging your entire wardrobe up and down those steps."

"Isn't there a bellboy?"

Rebecca pursed her lips. "No, this is someone's house. The

woman who greeted me is about a hundred years old, and I'm not going to ask her husband to carry our things."

Arabella visibly deflated. "Fine. But I need two bags, one is my makeup case."

Rebecca chuckled. "You need a *case* of makeup?"

"We can't all be twenty-seven."

She narrowed her eyes. "How do you know I'm twenty-seven?"

Arabella paused for a second. "You told me, during your incessant blathering on."

"Hey, I don't incessantly blather—"

"Don't just stand there, help me out of the car."

Arabella opened the passenger door and started to try to edge her way towards it. Rebecca shook her head. One moment Arabella was bordering on nice, the next she was as cutting as ever.

She held the door open as Arabella tried to pivot herself out of the vehicle. Rebecca frowned. Arabella had seemed pretty spry before, but now she appeared to be struggling. She assumed that it was something to do with being stuck in the same position for so many hours.

In a sudden burst of movement, Arabella launched herself up out of the car. Her crutch gave way on the shingled driveway and Arabella pitched forward. Rebecca quickly moved in and grabbed her by the upper arms to hold her up. Arabella panted hard at the shock of slipping and almost falling.

"Thank you," Arabella murmured.

"That's okay, I'm not staying in this place overnight by myself," Rebecca joked.

"Your concern for my wellbeing is heart-warming." Her tone was light.

Rebecca waited for Arabella to right herself and hold onto the top of the car. Once she was sure that she was steady, she bent down and grabbed the abandoned crutch.

"So, was she cleaning a meat cleaver with a bloodied rag when she opened the door?" Arabella asked.

Rebecca laughed. "Don't! I'll never get any sleep!"

"Good, one of us needs to keep an ear out for bumps in the night."

Arabella took the crutch from Rebecca and adjusted her stance. She let go of the car and pivoted to face her.

"Thank you," she mumbled again. "Shall we?"

Arabella bit her lip. She took in the decor while her host was away preparing tea and sandwiches. At first, she had just seen a very large but old-fashioned sitting room. Fabric wingback chairs and leather sofas. The kind of thing you would expect in an older property, especially one that welcomed guests on a regular basis.

Mary Davenport had led her in, treating her as if she were an invalid. She'd guided her to a wingback chair in front of the fire. As soon as Arabella had sat down, a footstool had been dragged across the room and her plaster-covered leg was being hoisted on top of it.

With the promise of fresh tea, Mary had left the room, which allowed Arabella the time to see the other occupants of the room: shelves upon shelves of porcelain dolls. Arabella had often visited houses of clients who were collectors. Sometimes their collections lived on the odd shelf throughout the home, sometimes an entire room was dedicated to it. But she'd never seen anything on this scale.

She guessed that there were at least two hundred dolls in the room. They were on shelves, on the coffee table, one even sat on the sofa. All of them stared at her. Their dead eyes looking right her.

Even the large Christmas tree in the corner of the room had a few smaller dolls hidden in the branches, like something out of a gardener's worse nightmare.

"Hey, you should see upstairs, Jesus." Rebecca stopped dead in the middle of the room and followed Arabella's gaze. "Oh, they're in here, too."

"They're upstairs?"

"Oh, they're *everywhere*," Rebecca told her. She pulled her leather jacket off, the heat from the fire making the room overwhelmingly hot. "They are on the stairs, like in the corners, ready to grab your ankles. On the landing. Sitting in chairs on the landing. On windowsills. On the second set of stairs, on the second landing."

Arabella bristled at the idea. She was suddenly even more pleased to have Rebecca with her.

"None of this was in the photographs online," Arabella said. "It just said charming bed and breakfast, not fog-obscured gothic mansion owned by geriatric doll-collecting maniac."

"Shh." Rebecca turned around to see if she could see their hosts.

"Have you seen the husband?" Arabella asked.

"No, why?"

"Do we know that there *is* a husband?"

Rebecca glared at her. "Stop, I'm already freaked out."

"I'm serious. I've only seen her. He's not upstairs?" Arabella tried to twist her body around so she could see the door. Only now was she wondering why her host had put her in a chair with her back to the door.

"Well, I didn't do a full search, but I didn't see him."

Arabella raised her eyebrow and remained silent.

Rebecca opened her mouth to speak but stopped as Mary entered the room again, a tea tray in her hands.

"Oh good, you're both here. I made some sandwiches. How are you both settling in?" Mary asked.

Arabella remained silent and looked at Rebecca, indicating that she was to answer.

"Very well. You have a lovely home," Rebecca replied.

Arabella nearly snorted a laugh but managed to stop herself just in time.

"And thank you so much for the sandwiches," Rebecca continued, glaring at Arabella while Mary busied herself with putting the tray onto a coffee table.

"You're very welcome; I'm afraid you'll struggle to find anywhere else to eat around here. We're a little out of the way," Mary said.

Arabella raised her eyebrow again and looked at Rebecca. Rebecca shook her head and rolled her eyes.

"Do you live here alone?" Arabella asked.

"No, with my husband, Jonathan."

"I look forward to meeting him," Arabella said.

"Oh, I'm sure he'll come and introduce himself at some point," Mary said. "I'll leave you girls to it, ring the bell if you need me."

Mary gestured towards an old-fashioned brass button by the fireplace. By the time Arabella looked away from the bell, Mary had gone.

Rebecca picked up the plate of sandwiches and offered it towards Arabella. She looked at it with a sigh.

"Yeah, I know it's not wholegrain, seeded rye bread with an avocado and hummus filling, but it will have to do," Rebecca told her.

Arabella was about to deny that was what she was thinking. But another look at the starchy white bread sandwich and she couldn't stop herself grimacing.

"Eat one," Rebecca pressed.

She picked up a sandwich and took a small bite. It wasn't too bad, even if it did remind her of the sandwiches she ate at school many years ago.

Rebecca moved the table nearer to them so they could both reach the tea and sandwiches. Rebecca sat down, kicked off her ankle-length boots, and started to wiggle her toes.

Arabella stared at the dolls. Mainly because they were staring at her. "Do you collect anything?"

"Not really."

"Not really sounds like you do but you don't want to admit to it," Arabella said.

"It's not really a collection, as such. But every time I do a new photoshoot, I take a test shot to check my settings. I always print and keep that test shot. Everyone gets to see the final shots that make it to print, but only I have those first images. They might be out of focus, too much ISO, too little, incorrect f-stop. Whatever. Sometimes they are fine. But it's something that only I have, and I like that."

Arabella smiled. It wasn't a collection in a traditional sense, it was documenting her own life. Like a visual work diary, a reminder of her projects. She could see the appeal; she had kept the particulars from the first properties she had ever sold.

"What about you?" Rebecca asked. "Do you collect anything?"

"Keys," Arabella replied. "Old keys. My grandmother had a rusty old key that she dug up in her garden, and I was absolutely fascinated with it. It was the kind of key that you draw when you were a child. Very simplistic, but big and important-looking. When I started working in the estate agency, it seemed an appropriate collection to keep."

"Sounds cool. I suppose you have keys that have a cool story and huge price tag attached." Rebecca picked up another sandwich.

"A few," she admitted. "I do have one that is the key to some of the shackles used in the Tower of London. Who knows what that key could say if it could talk."

"Shackles? Didn't think of you as the bondage type." Rebecca winked as she sipped tea.

Arabella laughed. "Oh, there's a lot you don't know about me, I'm sure." She returned the wink.

She enjoyed the back-and-forth banter she shared with Rebecca. It wasn't like the conversations she had with her friends. It was on the edge of being risqué, but she knew it was all in good humour. She didn't feel she had to watch what she said.

Rebecca snorted. She picked up the plate of sandwiches and held it out towards Arabella. She took another sandwich, only now realising how hungry she actually was.

"When's your wedding?" Rebecca asked.

"Soon." She took a large bite of the sandwich. The need for real food outweighed her knowledge of just how much sugar she was ingesting.

"Do you have everything sorted out and planned?"

"Most of it."

"Wow, you seem so excited," she said with a touch of sarcasm.

"Have you ever been married?" Arabella changed the subject.

"Nope."

"Been asked?" she fished.

"Nope."

"Asked someone?"

Rebecca hesitated a moment. Her cheeks started to show some colour.

"Aha," Arabella said knowingly. "So, what happened?"

Rebecca shrugged. "She said no. She said I was too young." She wiggled her toes and watched them, trying to look like she was unfazed by the fact. Trying, but failing.

"How old were you?"

"Twenty-three."

Arabella nodded. "You were too young."

Rebecca rolled her eyes and flopped back in her chair. "Wow, judgemental much?"

"Not judgemental, just older than you." She tossed the crust of her sandwich onto the plate. She wasn't about to completely destroy her waistline.

"So, because you're older than me, you automatically know better than me?"

"Yes, I'm an oracle. Like Yoda."

Rebecca laughed. Her irritation evaporated at the well-placed joke. "Don't tell me you watch *Star Wars*?"

"I may have seen it once or twice," Arabella confessed.

"Well, Yoda or not, just because you're older than me doesn't mean that you know better than me."

"Maybe," Arabella allowed. She lowered her cast from the footstool and leaned forward to prepare herself a cup of tea.

Suddenly something occurred to her. "You say that she said you were too young? So, how old was she?"

Rebecca's eyes drifted towards the fire. The blush that was light on her cheeks grew in richness and started to encompass her ears.

Interesting, Arabella thought.

"In her forties…"

Arabella nearly dropped the milk jug.

"Late… forties," Rebecca continued.

"How late?" Arabella asked, unable to stop herself.

"Nine," Rebecca whispered.

"You were twenty-three and she was forty-nine? That's… that's… twenty-six years difference. She was more than twice as old as you."

Rebecca shrugged. "I loved her, and she loved me."

"What happened?"

Rebecca tore her gaze away from the fire and reached for another sandwich. "She let me go. Her words. She said she loved me, and I know that she did. But she thought she was trapping me in a life where she would be growing older and older as I'd be coming into my prime. Again, her words.

"I wanted to prove to her that I loved her, that I'd stick by her. So, I proposed. But that was the beginning of the end. I thought that making that ultimate promise would be the proof that I didn't care about her age, that I just wanted to be with her. But it made her think about the future, what we were doing. And she broke up with me."

Arabella slowly stirred her tea, her mind racing in a hundred different directions at once. She couldn't imagine a twenty-three-year-old being in love with a forty-nine-year-old. Hell, she wasn't even sure she knew what love was herself.

"How did you know you loved her?"

Rebecca looked at her. "How do you know you love Alastair?"

"Humour me?" Arabella requested.

Rebecca let out a sigh and sat back in her seat. She brought her legs up, hugging her knees to her chest. "I enjoyed her company. Every moment we were together was something I enjoyed. I never spent a minute with her and thought it was a minute I would rather be doing something else. She made me laugh, made me think, made me hope, wish, dream. She listened to me, told me when I was wrong, agreed with me when I was right. We'd argue about things, not fight, just express a difference of opinion. Debate, I suppose. And we both learnt something new, about the subject, about ourselves, and about each other. I grew as a person, which is the purpose of life."

Arabella blinked. "Is it?"

Rebecca looked at her. "I think so. I would hate to think that I graduated university and then never changed. I had my opinions and that was that. I want to be challenged, I want to learn new things, I want to be more today than I was yesterday."

Arabella played with her necklace as she considered what Rebecca had said. She didn't have a pithy reply, nor a sarcastic comment. In fact, now she was left wondering if the scruffy, young photographer was right. Maybe Rebecca knew the purpose of life and she didn't.

"Look, I don't mean to be rude, but I have to go to bed," Rebecca said, she smothered a yawn with the back of her hand.

Arabella looked at her watch, suddenly remembering the reason for the stop.

"Of course, no problem."

"I told Mary that we'd be leaving at six, she said she would leave some breakfast out for us." Rebecca stood up and gathered her boots.

She stepped forward and handed Arabella a key.

"Your room is up the stairs and at the end on the left, it has a three on the door. I'm up the next flight of stairs at the top of the house. Will you be okay getting up there?"

Arabella took the key and nodded. "I'll be fine. But thank you."

"Okay, text me if you need anything."

"I will, goodnight."

"Night."

Rebecca picked up her jacket and walked out of the room.

Arabella let out a breath and leaned back, staring at the ceiling.

This trip was the journey from hell. Not because she was trapped in a house with a thousand creepy dolls, not because she should be home by now, and not because she was stuck with someone she hardly knew.

It was hell because it was giving her time to think. Something she had been avoiding for weeks. But miles of staring at nothing left little time for anything but reflective thought.

She knew that she didn't love Alastair, and that he didn't love her.

Not really.

Not in the true sense of love. But it had never mattered before. Getting married was just a formality, a step in the process of life. She knew it was her lot in life to get married, stop working, have children, be a mother, and… that was it. It was what the women in her family did.

Some juggled a career and being a parent, but Alastair and her own father had been adamantly against that. They wanted Arabella to stay home. Staying at home would be about as much work as going to an office. There would be coffee mornings, luncheons, dinner parties, charitable balls, and all other kinds of events to organise. Alastair had even joked that she was technically changing career from an estate agent to a party planner.

Arabella didn't want to be a party planner, but it was too late now. The wedding was fast approaching, announcements had been made and invitations had been sent.

Everyone knew.

To pull out now would be embarrassing, to say the least. And then what would she do? If it wasn't Alastair, it would be someone else. While Alastair wasn't perfect, he wasn't as bad as some that had gone before him.

She sighed again.

It was just this damn trip that was giving her doubts. Rebecca and her strange outlook on life were shaking everything up. Rebecca seemed to live in a dream world. A world where people were endlessly kind and respectful of one another. Where love existed, outside of fairy tales and Disney movies.

She's a creative, they're always a little odd, Arabella reminded herself.

She was young and naive. In a few years, she'd be married to someone who wasn't the love of her life, just someone who fit the role. Just like everyone else.

"Has your friend gone to bed?"

Arabella looked up to see Mary had entered the room.

"Yes, she's been doing a lot of driving, she's very tired."

"She said all the way from Portugal? It's a very long way. And back to England before Christmas?"

"Hopefully," Arabella said.

"Make sure you book yourself on a ferry, they do become quite booked up."

"I plan to do it in the morning before we set off," Arabella reassured her.

"Oh, good. It is so important to get back home for Christmas, isn't it? I'm sure you both have a lot of people expecting you?"

Arabella thought of the Christmas Eve party, filled with people all wanting to talk to her about business or gossip about other partygoers. Then she thought of Rebecca, seemingly going home just to spend Christmas with her mother. Planning to watch the same shows they watched every year, eat the same things they ate every year. Both heading home for Christmas traditions, but both so widely different from each other.

"Yes, lots of people," Arabella answered. "Will you be spending Christmas here?"

"We will, we invite the locals and we have a big Christmas dinner. It's a mix of French and British foods and traditions. I thought I'd never break with my British traditions, but, I have to say, the French tradition of eating oysters at Christmas is something I really enjoy. Sometimes you need to mix things up a bit, keep things fresh."

Arabella smiled.

Here she was, judging some elderly lady with her probably make-believe husband and her ten thousand porcelain dolls, who goes on to have a more well-rounded view on Christmas traditions. Willing to accept changes, even at her later stage in life.

"That sounds lovely," Arabella said diplomatically. She was too tired and too fragile to have any more personal conversations. She just wanted to go to bed and wake up feeling different. The exhaustion and stress of travel were causing her to question decisions that could not be questioned. She knew that with some sleep and some time, she would be back to normal.

"I better get some sleep as well," she said. "Thank you so much for the tea and the sandwiches, they were very much appreciated."

"Of course, my dear." Mary looked at her foot. "Will you be all right with the stairs?"

"Absolutely." Arabella picked up her crutch and stood up. "It's just a minor fracture, hardly the need for a full cast, but the doctor wanted to be safe."

Mary didn't seem satisfied with the response and continued to look at her with a sympathetic expression. Arabella hated appearing weak, especially in front of strangers.

"Well, good night," she said. She quickly made her way to the door, ignoring the twinge of pain that rushed up her leg at the sudden movement.

CHAPTER 11

REBECCA CHANGED LANES. She used the opportunity of looking in her wing mirror to glance at Arabella. The woman had been quiet since they'd left the that morning. Something seemed to be up.

Rebecca wondered if the creepy porcelain dolls in her bedroom had prevented her from sleeping. Rebecca had been certain that she'd not be able to sleep when she'd seen the countless dolls, but she'd been so exhausted that she'd quickly fallen into a deep slumber. Maybe Arabella hadn't been so lucky.

But it seemed Arabella wasn't about to admit to anything. She'd told Rebecca that she'd slept fine when she'd enquired over breakfast. Since then, it had been four hours of polite comments and very stilted conversation.

Eventually, Rebecca had given up, not wanting to push Arabella who clearly didn't want to talk to her.

She was surprised that she cared so much about the silence. They'd had periods of silence in the car before, but this felt different. She could feel that something was on Arabella's mind.

The car was thick with the emotion radiating off of the older woman.

Arabella's phone rang. The atmosphere became impossibly thicker.

"It's Alastair," Arabella announced after glancing at the screen.

"Are you going to answer it?" Rebecca asked. "I'd try to give you some privacy, but... you know. I suppose I could find somewhere to stop?"

"No, it's fine, I... I'll take the call."

Rebecca tightened her grip on the steering wheel, attempting to focus more fully on the road and ignore what was happening beside her. She hated that such a strong and independent woman could be reduced to an uncertain bag of nerves by some *man*. Especially some man that she was due to marry.

"Hello, Alastair," Arabella answered the call.

Rebecca could hear mumbling on the other end of the call. At least this time he sounded calmer. While she couldn't make out the words, she could tell that his speech pattern was slower and softer.

"We're a little more than halfway through France..."

Rebecca looked at the GPS screen. It was true, they were halfway through France. It was Christmas Eve, but they were well on their way. They'd get there just before Christmas Day, but they would make it.

"Well, we stopped overnight." Arabella's tone became defensive. "Because we couldn't drive solidly." She paused and sighed. "The hire company wouldn't let me drive at all because of my leg, so I'm relying on my travel companion."

There was a long pause.

"They literally wouldn't allow me to drive. Something about

invalidating insurance," Arabella explained. "Well, I suppose I *could* have…"

Rebecca knew what he was saying without hearing him. He was suggesting that Arabella should have driven through the night. How anyone could suggest that was beyond her.

She'd seen the winces, the tightened facial expressions. Whether or not Arabella wanted to admit to it, she was in pain from sitting so long in one position. Driving would only exacerbate that. How could someone who supposedly loved her suggest that she put her life in danger by driving through the night?

"What's done is done," Arabella was saying to Alistair. "We'll be there before the midnight toast."

Rebecca winced at the sound of the raised voice on the other end of the line. Alastair was clearly not happy with that predicted timeline.

"There's not a lot I can do now. We're getting a ferry in a few hours and then we'll be driving up from Dover. I think we'll be at the house between nine and ten. It's the best I can do, Alastair."

Rebecca smirked at the firm tone that Arabella had used.

Clearly, she did have some backbone when talking to the man.

Arabella sighed. "They'll have to accept me as I am, I'm afraid. I can't exactly do my hair in the car, can I?"

Rebecca felt her jaw drop open.

She looked at Arabella and shook her head in shock before looking back at the road. She couldn't believe the audacity of the man. He couldn't just be satisfied that Arabella would be home in time, he had to comment on what state she would arrive in?

Not that Rebecca could ever imagine Arabella looking less than perfect. Despite the long journey, the pain in her leg, and the lack of rest, Arabella had appeared at breakfast looking stunning. Another skirt suit, hair styled, makeup applied.

Rebecca had immediately felt tiny in comparison. Until Arabella had commented that she looked well rested. The small compliment had oddly sent her heart soaring.

"Yes, I have calculated the hour time difference, I'm not a complete idiot," Arabella argued.

Rebecca smiled. Maybe Arabella was going to be okay with Alastair after all. Maybe yesterday she was at a low ebb and now she was back to full power, ready to tell him what's what.

"Fine, fine, I'll do my best, but don't expect me before nine. Please tell Daddy. Goodbye, Alastair." Arabella angrily stabbed the end call button and let out a sigh.

Rebecca tried to relax herself back into her chair.

Since the start of the call, her body had tensed. She took a couple of deep breaths, brought her shoulders down away from her ears, and released her grip on the steering wheel a little. She couldn't tell if it was general conflict that made her uncomfortable or the thought of Alastair himself. She'd taken an instant dislike to him based on the one phone call Arabella had previously had with him. She knew nothing of the man, other than he seemed like an old-fashioned fossil who didn't really care about Arabella at all.

Not that any of that should matter.

It wasn't like Arabella was anything to her. They were simply sharing a journey home, nothing more and nothing less. Travel companion, that's what Arabella had called her. In a few hours, they would part ways and then they would probably never see nor hear from each other ever again. This was just a strange twist of fate.

She looked at the GPS screen again. Arabella had programmed in the port as their destination. That way they could see if they would, in fact, make it to the ferry.

So far, everything looked good, but Rebecca knew that one heavy batch of traffic could change everything. The thought of missing the ferry caused a cold sweat to break out. She needed to get that ferry, she needed to get home.

"Rebecca?"

She blinked, shaking herself out of her thoughts. "What?"

"You're speeding. Quite a lot." Arabella didn't sound angry, just surprised.

Rebecca looked down at the speed display. She took her foot off of the accelerator and applied the brake.

"I didn't know you had it in you," Arabella said.

"I didn't mean to." Rebecca watched the speedometer like a hawk. Once it was down to the correct speed, she released a breath. Her eyes flicked up to the rear-view mirror, something had caught her eye.

"Shit," she murmured.

"What?" Arabella asked.

Rebecca gripped the steering wheel tightly. She indicated and started to slow down and pull over. "The police are behind us."

Arabella turned to look behind them. "Oh, for god's sake, we don't have time for this."

"I know." Rebecca indicated and started to pull over.

"The one time you decide to speed, you do it in front of a *police car?*"

"I didn't do it on purpose! I didn't even know I was speeding."

"Then maybe you shouldn't be driving!"

Rebecca pulled the car over onto the hard shoulder. Her heart was beating out of her chest. She'd never driven over the speed limit. She'd never been pulled over by police. The one time she got distracted and allowed her lead foot to drift over the speed limit, she was being flagged down. She had no idea what to do, what to say. What was about to happen.

"This is ridiculous, we don't have time," Arabella was saying. "I can't believe you were foolish enough to—"

"Just stop," Rebecca sighed. "Okay? Please? Just stop. You can scream and shout all the way to Calais, once they let us go."

Arabella let out a long sigh and folded her arms. She turned her head to look out of the passenger window.

Rebecca took a deep breath and watched as the police officer approached the car.

CHAPTER 12

ARABELLA GRABBED hold of her handbag, ready to get out of the car and away from Rebecca as soon as she could. The debacle with the French police had taken over forty minutes. She'd counted each minute, gradually becoming more frustrated as each ticked away.

They had laboriously wanted to check every single detail of every piece of paperwork. They'd even phoned England to see if everything was in order with Rebecca's licence. On Christmas Eve, which had obviously taken ages.

Luckily, they had *just* managed to catch the ferry. After five hours of driving in complete silence. They'd stopped once for fuel and to get some food, a stop that would have made any Formula 1 pit manager proud.

Rebecca had wisely chosen to stay silent throughout the journey, clearly sensing the anger radiating from Arabella. The few times the girl had tried to say anything, Arabella simply held her hand up to silence her. Shaking her head to indicate that now was not the time.

She still couldn't believe that the girl was idiotic enough to endanger their entire journey by speeding, right next to a police car. And then panic when questioned by the police, stuttering and making them look suspicious when she couldn't answer basic questions. The whole thing was a delay and extra stress that they didn't need.

The ferry staff directed them towards their bay. The very second the car had come to a stop, Arabella unclipped her seatbelt and reached for the door handle.

"Hey, where are you going?" Rebecca asked.

Arabella paused and turned to face her. "I need some time on my own. If that's quite okay with you?"

Rebecca sighed. "Are you still angry about the police? I apologised so many times, I didn't mean—"

Arabella opened the car door and got out. She leant against the car and reached for her crutch. Rebecca was around the car in a few moments, trying to help.

"I'm perfectly capable of doing this myself," Arabella bit out. "What do you think I did before you came along?"

"I'm just trying to help," Rebecca argued.

"Help by getting me home."

"I am."

Arabella grabbed her crutch and pivoted away from the car, slamming the door behind her. She started to walk away, keen to get some distance from Rebecca.

But Rebecca didn't seem to understand and was following her.

"Look, I apologised. I don't know what else you want me to do."

Arabella spun around. "I expect you to think of someone else for a change. I need to get home, I need to be at this party.

It may seem silly to you, but it's my life. Just because you want to hurry home to eat Christmas cake with your mum, that doesn't mean I expect you to jeopardise my journey home."

"So, you getting home to get to your family is more important?" Rebecca stepped close. "Is that what you're saying?"

Arabella stood tall. "Yes, I am."

Rebecca stared at her for a long, silent moment. "Fuck you, Arabella." She turned and walked away.

"Oh, very mature!" Arabella called after her.

She continued towards the ferry's elevator to get away from the car deck and into some fresh air. She jabbed the button and waited. She couldn't believe that the girl had spoken to her like that. On a crowded ferry, too.

When the lift arrived, she stepped in and quickly selected the top deck. The doors slid closed and she leaned against the wall of the tiny elevator.

Rebecca was just as childish and naive as she thought she was when she first met her. Assuming the girl had a grain of intelligence had obviously been a mistake. If she couldn't see that her actions had the potential to jeopardise their entire trip, then Arabella didn't know how she could explain it to her.

From the moment the police let them on their way, with a hefty fine, they had been against the clock. Unable to race along for fear of other police officers seeing them. Being stopped once was one matter, being stopped again was entirely different. They wouldn't get off so lightly if they were stopped again. If you could call forty minutes' inquisition light.

And so, they were forced to obey the speed limit. The whole debacle was ridiculously stressful. And why? Because Rebecca had made a stupid mistake. She was supposed to be helping

Arabella get home, not sabotaging her from ever getting there. She momentarily imagined herself stuck in a French prison.

The elevator doors opened and shook her from the thought.

She walked out and looked around. To her left was a large restaurant with large forward-facing windows. To her right was a shop and a grubby-looking casino. Directly in front of her were doors leading to the deck. A woman wearing a hideous sweater with a large Christmas tree on the front stood on the deck. She looked frozen and had one hand on the Santa hat atop her head, keeping it in place despite the strong winds.

Arabella shook her head and walked into the restaurant. She stopped in the doorway. The place was crammed with people. The sound of everyone speaking, laughing, even singing, was deafening. She turned and left the restaurant again.

She eyed the door to the deck. It may be cold, but at least it was quiet.

She wrapped her coat around her and walked out onto the deck.

The cold winter air hit her immediately, but it wasn't as unpleasant as she thought it would be. Being cooped up in a car for so many hours had given her a greater appreciation of fresh air. She walked a little until she found a set of moulded plastic seats bolted to the deck. She lowered herself into a chair and stared out at the bustling docks.

She was still angry at Rebecca for swearing at her. That had been completely uncalled for. Just because she wasn't ready to accept an apology for the girl's ridiculous lack of judgement didn't mean she deserved to be shouted at.

She turned and looked in through the windows, wondering if she could spot Rebecca anywhere. Not that she cared where the girl was. She just wanted to avoid a second round of arguing. She turned a little more, squinting as she looked into the restaurant. She hoped Rebecca would have the common sense to get a proper meal, she couldn't continue the journey on just sweets.

Arabella turned back and looked at her watch. She couldn't believe it was Christmas Eve. She was supposed to be at home, preparing for the party. Right now, she should be reconsidering her choice of outfit. She'd soon be on her way to her hair appointment, then to get her nails done. Of course, she'd be on the phone with the event planner endlessly, fixing any last-minute issues.

She felt a pull to pick up her phone and text Alastair about some of the finer party details that she was sure he would forget. But she knew that would just invite criticism as to her absence. No, he would have to deal with it all himself. She might be on her way to being a housewife who dealt with those issues, but she wasn't quite there yet. He'd have to manage this one alone.

She twisted herself around again, looking for Rebecca. She wondered if the girl was aware that she wasn't allowed to be on the car deck when the ferry departed. She wouldn't put it past her to stubbornly try to sit in the car for the hour and a half journey. She wondered if she should call her. Or ask a member of staff to check on her.

She turned back to face the dock. She didn't know why she even cared.

Sure, Rebecca had the keys to car. But if she decided to leave without her once they were in Dover, Arabella could pay a taxi driver to take her home if needed. It wasn't like she needed Rebecca any more.

She stood up, readjusting her crutch as she peered back into the ferry.

She didn't *need* Rebecca any longer, but it would be the simpler choice to continue as they were rather than find an alternative method of transportation.

After a few moments she realised it was futile, there were too many people and she'd never be able to pick out Rebecca in the crowd. Especially if, as she suspected, the girl didn't want to be found. She sat back down again and let out a sigh. Soon this nightmare trip would be over.

***

Once the ferry had started to move, the temperatures had taken a dramatic dive and the wind had increased tenfold. Arabella knew that the sea air would play havoc with her hair, and she had to be at a party in a few hours. There was only so much that dry shampoo could do.

She'd gone inside and walked around the decks, feeling relief at being able to stretch her injured leg. After a while, she'd found a quieter deck, one with mainly seating and had walked slow laps.

Before she knew it, the ferry was slowing. The white cliffs of Dover could just be seen through the forward windows, despite the setting sun.

Somehow, she had managed to walk for ninety minutes without realising it. Her thoughts had been tied up with the party, her future, and, for some reason, Rebecca.

She hated that the girl was so prominent in her thoughts. It was hard to get her out of her mind, surely the result of having spent so much time with her recently. And the result of her flip-flopping personality. One minute she was a petulant child in a car hire offer, preventing her from getting the vehicle. The next she was thoughtful, kind, and maybe even funny. The next she was cursing at her aboard a ferry.

She really didn't know what to make of her.

After what felt like an endless wait, the ferry finally docked at Dover. The captain announced that the stairs and elevators to the lower decks were now open. A swarm of people rushed past her, desperate to be the first down the stairs. Not that it mattered. They'd all have to wait for everyone to be in their cars anyway.

Arabella hated herd mentality.

She queued for the elevator, finally getting in on the eighth journey, sandwiched between two prams of screaming children. She wondered if maybe she should've stayed at Faro and waited for the flights to start again. Surely that would have been better than the situation she found herself in now?

Finally, she escaped the elevator and the children. She looked around to get her bearings, still not seeing Rebecca anywhere. Her heart beat a little faster as she worried that the girl had fallen overboard or was maybe stuck in one of the ridiculously small toilets with their spring-loaded doors.

She hurried towards the rental car, looking in as she arrived. There she was. Sitting at the wheel, like nothing had happened.

Arabella opened the door and got in. She adjusted her crutch, surprised that Rebecca didn't help as she had done all of the other times. *Showing her true colours now.*

"Are you going to apologise?" Arabella asked bitterly. She slammed the door shut.

"No. And I don't think we have anything else to say to each other," Rebecca said.

Arabella fidgeted with her seatbelt. "So, what? You expect us to sit in silence for the next two hours?"

"That sounds preferable."

Arabella looked at the girl in surprise. She sat bolt upright, focused straight ahead. Her cheeks were flushed, and she wore her sunglasses despite it being almost dark outside.

Has she been crying? she wondered.

"Fine," Arabella said.

"Good," Rebecca replied coldly.

CHAPTER 13

TRUE TO HER WORD, Rebecca didn't say a word for the entire journey to Putney.

She almost spoke up as they passed the turning for Croydon. She wondered briefly if she could stop and leave Arabella to make her way home. But she'd made a deal with Arabella. As much as she wanted to be out of the car, she knew that Arabella shouldn't be driving. Especially after sitting in one position for so long, her leg must have been in agony.

She'd never forgive herself if the older woman got into an accident on the way to Putney. So, she continued on. An hour away from Croydon. Where she wanted to be. Where she needed to be. And from Putney, she'd drop the car off and somehow make her own way back.

Arabella had been on her phone for the majority of the trip back. The incessant sound of text messages arriving had started to irritate Rebecca, but she got the impression that that was part of Arabella's idea, to attempt to irritate Rebecca enough to speak.

She'd also become suddenly fascinated with the window controls and the car climate control system. Opening and closing windows and adjusting the temperature from hot to cold to hot again.

Seemingly anything to get something out of her. Not that Rebecca was going to fall for such childish ploys.

She just kept driving. Even though she was exhausted, even though her eyes rotated from being painfully dry to just too tired to keep open. Even though her legs were numb from sitting in the same position for so many hours. Even though she was hungry and thirsty, she kept driving. The sooner this was all over, the sooner she could get on with her life.

Arabella had reprogrammed the GPS to go directly to her home address. Rebecca continually looked at the screen, counting down the minutes. She felt sweet relief when the ETA dropped to under an hour. She felt almost euphoric when the time dropped to the single digits.

"This one on the left, just park outside," Arabella said as the clock hit one minute.

Rebecca looked up at the large white wall and open gates. As she had suspected, it was a mansion. Cars lined the drive inside the gates as well as the outside street. The lights gleamed through the windows, through which she could clearly see people drinking from champagne flutes.

"Looks like you made it to your party," Rebecca commented dryly.

"Yes, though I'll have to slip in the back way so I can get ready. Can't have anyone seeing me like this."

Rebecca blinked. "Why not? You look great."

Arabella looked at her for a moment, her expression clearly showing that she was torn between accepting the compliment and making a snide remark about the end of the silent treatment.

Before she could make her decision, Rebecca saw a man appear by the side of the car and tap on the window. Arabella jumped and turned around to see what the noise was.

She opened the car door.

"Alastair, thank goodness," she said.

"Come on, before anyone sees you." He looked in the car at Rebecca. "Thanks for driving her."

"You're welcome," Rebecca mumbled.

Yes, as she suspected, she hated him. He was a little older than Arabella. She supposed he'd be considered classically handsome. He wore a tuxedo well enough. But Rebecca hated him on sight.

She quickly turned off the engine and got out of the car. She opened the back door and threw her rucksack over her shoulder. She closed both of the doors and held out the car key for Arabella.

"There you go, enjoy your party." She turned to leave.

"Wait!" Arabella called.

Rebecca paused and slowly turned around.

Arabella whispered something to Alastair. He nodded and left. Arabella walked towards Rebecca, eyeing her up and down as she did.

"Well, that was an interesting trip. Thank you for driving me, I wouldn't have made it back here without you."

"I know. Is that it?" She folded her arms.

Arabella sighed. "No, it's not. I ordered you a taxi, it will be here in a moment."

"You... what? Why?"

"You'll never be able to get a taxi at this time of night on

Christmas Eve and I'm sure public transport will be horrible. It's all paid for, you don't need to worry about that."

Rebecca licked her lips. "Oh... I..."

She didn't know what to say.

She didn't expect any kindness from Arabella considering how she had treated her on the final leg of their journey. Even if she had deserved it, Arabella hadn't known *why* she deserved it. Arabella didn't know why Rebecca was rushing home.

"Thank you," Rebecca finally said. She stood awkwardly, not wanting to make eye contact.

Arabella looked at her phone. "He's just around the corner, he'll be here in a moment."

"Okay." Rebecca looked up, eager to see headlights and her escape route.

"So, I'll say goodnight. Again, thank you." Arabella seemed rooted to the spot, unwilling to leave just yet.

Probably waiting for a thank-you in return.

Rebecca looked up at her. "You're welcome. Thanks for paying for the car. And everything. I really appreciate it."

It was true, she did appreciate it. Even if she had wanted to kill Arabella on the ferry.

Arabella smiled. "Merry Christmas."

A car pulled up beside them. "Rebecca Edwards?" the driver called out of the open window.

Rebecca held her hand up to indicate she was coming. "Merry Christmas, enjoy your party."

Arabella chuckled. "Oh, these parties aren't for enjoyment. But I'll do my best. Goodbye, Rebecca."

"Bye, Arabella."

Rebecca watched as Arabella turned and walked through the gate. It felt weird to say goodbye. She'd never see Arabella again.

Unless she suddenly won the lottery and wanted to buy a property in Portugal. But Arabella would probably have quit work by then if Alastair had his way.

She turned and walked towards the taxi. She got into the back seat, relieved not to be driving any more.

The driver wore a Santa hat.

"Merry Christmas," he greeted.

"Merry Christmas," she replied.

"Croydon, right?"

"That's right."

"Rosemont Avenue?"

Rebecca frowned as she wondered how Arabella knew her home address. She shook her head, it was irrelevant now.

"Actually no, change of plan. It's near there, though…"

CHAPTER 14

Arabella sat at her makeup table, styling her hair. Luckily no one had seen her enter the back door of the house and make her way to the guest bedroom. Now she just needed to make herself as presentable as possible, get changed, and make an appearance downstairs.

The door flew open, and Alastair entered the bedroom.

She regarded him in the mirror. He met her eyes, and she could tell he was furious.

"How long do you think you'll be? I've been making excuses all night."

"Why did you make excuses? Surely the air traffic failure was in the news?"

Alastair snorted a laugh and sat on the edge of the bed.

"Like I'm going to tell people that you were stranded in Portugal so close to Christmas."

She spun around and looked at him. "Why ever not?"

He rolled his eyes. "Because that just screams poor time management. And people will ask why you were there and why we didn't send a junior, you know, like I suggested in the first place."

"I wanted to go," Arabella ground out.

"I know, and look how that ended up." He got to his feet and gestured for her to face the mirror again, eager for her to hurry in her preparations.

She sighed and turned around. She sought him out in the mirror and watched as he paced behind her.

"That's very distracting," she informed him.

He paused and met her eyes again. He folded his arms. "I hope you got it out of your system?"

"Got what out of my system?"

"Ignoring me, ignoring my advice. This need to always go it alone and do things yourself. If we're going to get married, I need to know that you'll listen to what I say. I don't mean that in a nasty way, I don't mean I'm the boss. I just mean that sometimes you should listen to me. Sometimes I know what's best."

"Best for who, Alastair?"

"Best for us. Best for the business."

She broke eye contact, picked up her lip gloss, and leaned closer to the mirror.

"I suppose I'm just struggling to understand why my stepping aside from the business is what's best for the business."

"I don't mean that," he argued. "Don't twist my words. We agreed that it would be better for you to be at home and me at the office. A division of labour. You know I can't sit in ladies' coffee mornings and persuade those women to persuade their husbands to put their rental business with us. And it's not just coffee mornings, it's charity events, balls, auctions... they need to be organised and it's just not a man's job. You know that."

A knock on the door stopped Arabella from delivering the argument that was on the tip of her tongue.

She turned to face the door. "Yes?"

Her father entered the room and smiled at her. "You're back."

"I am." She returned the smile. "Sorry I'm late, Daddy."

"You're here now, that's the main thing. Will you be down soon?"

She nodded. "In a few moments."

"Wonderful." He turned his attention to Alastair. "Come on, Alastair, there's some people I need to introduce you to."

Arabella let out a sigh of relief when they both left the room. She stretched out her back and turned her head from side to side to release the pressure. Sitting in a car seat for so long hadn't done her back any favours. Her eyes flicked to the small clock on the dressing table. She wondered if Rebecca was nearly home.

She returned her attention to applying her lip gloss. She really didn't know why she was wasting another moment thinking about the girl. She needed to forget about her and focus on the party.

CHAPTER 15

ARABELLA WALKED into the kitchen and politely smiled at the waitress who was pouring champagne into glasses. She hurried through and into the utility room, closing the door firmly behind her.

She placed her crutch by the wall and leaned against the door, hoping to have a moment to herself. She had no idea what was wrong with her. Usually, she enjoyed the Christmas party.

But this one was torturous.

Probably because people kept talking about the wedding and her stepping down from the firm.

She heard a light knock on the door and froze in fear.

"Arabella?"

She sighed with relief and took a step back to open the door. She gestured for her best friend to hurry in.

Miranda walked in. "Why are we hiding in the utility room?"

Arabella closed the door and leaned on it again. "I can't take it."

Miranda rested against the washing machine and sipped from her champagne glass. A perfectly manicured eyebrow rose questioningly.

"Can't take what, exactly?"

"All the talk about the wedding. People asking who will be looking after my work accounts. Asking about babies and telling me how lucky I am to have a man like Alastair. I can't take it."

She sucked in a deep breath.

Miranda frowned. She put her glass on the worktop and took Arabella by the upper arms.

"Take some deep breaths. I'm sure you're just exhausted, driving home... even if you weren't actually the one doing the driving... must have been exhausting."

"That's not it." Arabella shook her head. "It's all this, all these people telling me how excited I must be about quitting work. But I'm not. I love working—"

"And you'll love being a wife. It's a different kind of work," Miranda reassured.

She shrugged out of Miranda's grip. It was her turn to take her friend by the shoulders.

"Miranda, listen to what I'm saying. I don't want to quit work. I'm not looking forward to my own wedding."

She stared at Miranda meaningfully.

She watched as Miranda's eyes widened in understanding.

"Okay," her friend said solemnly. "Okay, but I don't think you should make any rash decisions now. You're tired, stressed, it's Christmas. You don't want to say or do something you might regret."

Arabella allowed her arms to drop to her sides. She leaned back against the door. Miranda was right. Making a hasty decision now could have potentially disastrous repercussions. While she felt certain at the moment, who was to say her feelings wouldn't change in a few hours?

She was exhausted. Sleep had been in short supply over the last few days and her stress levels had been ridiculously high.

"I'm just saying, take some time to think about it," Miranda continued. "Go through the motions. Give yourself some time to really think about what you're doing. If you pull the plug on you and Alastair now, there might not be any going back."

Arabella chuckled bitterly. "Aren't you supposed to be telling me what a great catch he is?"

Miranda took a step back and picked up her champagne glass.

"Let's be honest, neither of us were ever the kind of people who believed in love. We both knew that marriage would be about finding someone pleasant on the eyes and someone you could stand to spend the next ten or so years with."

Arabella swallowed. Even the idea of spending ten years with Alastair wasn't appealing to her at the moment.

"For us, marriage is more of a business transaction than anything else. Alastair obviously brings a lot of money and investment capital to Henley Estates. Which makes the business happy and your father happy. It makes Alastair and his family happy. Does it make you happy?"

Arabella threw her hands up in the air for a moment. "I don't know. It did. I thought it did. But now... I'm not so sure. Aren't we supposed to be a partnership, working together? It feels like I'm being pushed to one side to support him as his career grows. It's like I'm losing my identity. But then, I have to wonder if my happiness is worth more than everyone else's?"

"Yes," Miranda said firmly. "Darling, if we were having this conversation in the 1950s then I'd be telling you to pull yourself together and get on with it. But this is the twenty-first century. We're not subservient to men anymore. We're our own people. And your happiness is just as important as everyone else's."

Arabella let out another sigh. She looked down at the floor and shook her head. "What do I do?"

"You need a bit of breathing space. But I don't think hiding out in the utility room is going to work for long," Miranda said.

Right again. Arabella felt a tightness in her chest. Each time she heard someone moving in the kitchen she felt sure her refuge was about to be discovered.

Suddenly an idea struck her.

She snapped her head up and looked at Miranda. "Can you cover for me?"

"Sure, what's the plan?"

"I'm going to head outside for a bit. Catch my breath."

Miranda smiled warmly. "Good, take some time. Don't make any big decisions now. Get the holiday season out of the way and see how you feel then."

Arabella nodded. "I will, thank you."

They exchanged a quick hug, and Miranda left the utility room to return to the party.

After a few moments, Arabella took a fortifying breath and left the room, too. She headed towards her father's study where she'd dropped off her handbag. She grabbed the bag and waited for a quiet moment before slipping out of the back door of the house.

She crept around the side of the property, cursing the gravelled driveway beneath her crutch. She hoped no one would notice her painfully slow escape.

She walked out of the gate and towards the hire car, still sitting where Rebecca had parked it.

She unlocked the car and slipped into the driver's seat. She closed the door again. After a few moments, the interior light started to dim, and she sat in the darkness.

Hiding from her own party.

She tossed her handbag onto the passenger seat. What she thought of as *her* seat. She looked around the inside of the car. Flashes of memories from their journey came back to her. When she had ordered Rebecca to get her luggage, when they had listened to Spanish dance music, when they had stopped at the most beautiful vista Arabella had ever seen.

Getting stuck in Portugal hadn't been a part of her plan, but it had happened. And it had changed her. Shaking her from her daily routine long enough to stop and think about her life, where it was heading.

Since leaving university, life had been a conveyor belt. Her work, her future, all mapped out along the belt. She'd never realised before that it was possible to step off the conveyor. Everything had always been planned. She used to feel like she was the one planning it, but now she was beginning to wonder.

She shifted to try to find a more comfortable position. As she did, she felt something beneath her foot. She looked into the dark footwell and frowned. She leant forward and felt around the carpeted area. Her hand gripped something, something plastic and hard.

She lifted it up and held it towards the streetlight to see what she'd found. She turned the piece of plastic over and saw that it was a lens cap from a camera.

Rebecca must have dropped it, she thought.

She gripped the lens cap in her hand. She bit her lip and looked towards the house.

She'll need this, her lens is probably very expensive. It might get damaged, she thought.

Escape seemed very appealing.

She knew it was an excuse. She wanted just an hour or two away from the party to gather her thoughts, and this was the perfect excuse. She unlocked her phone and accessed the photo she had taken of Rebecca's driving licence. She started the engine and input the address into the GPS.

CHAPTER 16

ARABELLA PULLED up outside the house, only now realising that her knowing the address would take some explaining.

She looked out of the car window. Rebecca, it seemed, lived in a standard 1930s semi-detached, similar to thousands of other government-built homes on the outskirts of London. Outskirts that were now considered a part of the city itself. The houses weren't much to look at, but they were highly sought after and often high in value as London became more congested and popular.

Arabella frowned. The house looked empty. The lights were off, the curtains open, revealing no sign of life. Maybe this was Rebecca's house, but the girl was with her mother somewhere else?

Although, she wondered if a jobbing photographer could afford the high Croydon property prices, even to rent.

If the property were occupied, maybe it was just the front lights that were off. Maybe the family were gathered in a room in the back.

The lens cap wouldn't deliver itself. Arabella decided it was time to be brave and get out of the car and ring the bell.

She opened the door and shouldered her bag. She awkwardly adjusted her crutch and started to walk up the garden path. Her work instincts kicked in and she started to examine the garden, noting that it was unkempt. Clearly Rebecca's mother wasn't very green-fingered. She approached the front door, noting the slight peeling paintwork on the wooden frame as she rang the bell.

"Are you looking for Allison?"

Arabella turned around to see the neighbour leaning on the short garden fence. He wore a ridiculous Christmas sweater emblazoned with a snowman.

"Actually, I'm looking for Rebecca?"

"I've not seen her for a few days, she'll probably be up at the hospital with her mum."

"Hospital?"

He frowned, his face suddenly a stark contrast from his jovial sweater. "Oh, you don't know? Allison took a bad turn a couple of weeks ago. They didn't think she'd last the night, but she's a fighter. Scary how it can come back, isn't it? One moment you're in remission and the next..." He shuddered.

"Yes, frightening," Arabella agreed.

The ground felt shaky beneath her feet. Her constant nagging to get home for a work party suddenly seemed pathetic. Rebecca was racing home to her sick mother. And she hadn't said a word about it.

"Anyway, she's up at the Royal Victoria."

"Thank you," Arabella said softly.

She started back towards the car. Her mind was spinning as she analysed conversations they had shared on the drive home.

Some fresh perspective on Rebecca's words made her rethink so many of her assumptions about the girl. A girl who was going through so much, seemingly on her own.

"Merry Christmas," the neighbour called out.

"Merry Christmas," Arabella called over her shoulder without much heart in it.

She got into the car and threw her crutch into the passenger footwell. She remembered Rebecca's implosion on the ferry. Suddenly it seemed very clear why she had acted the way she had. Arabella had practically told her that her Christmas party was more important than Rebecca getting home to her mother. With no idea that her mother was sick, dying by the sound of it.

"So stupid," she mumbled to herself.

How had she shared so much time with Rebecca and not known something so important about her? Rebecca had obviously not wanted to discuss the matter. But Arabella couldn't help but feel that if she had tried a little harder to connect, she might have noticed something was up.

But she'd been so swept up in her own drama that she hadn't given a second thought to Rebecca's life. Getting home to the party and dealing with Alastair's inevitable sulk had been her entire focus.

She'd assumed that Rebecca was worrying about getting back to her mother to put on a ridiculous party hat and eat a Christmas cupcake, nothing more.

She wondered why Rebecca hadn't said anything.

She felt cold at the knowledge that she knew for sure that she would have. She would have instantly mentioned her dying mother to anyone in earshot. Not for sympathy, but to expedite her way home. If she felt that playing the dying parent card would have got her the hire car, she would have used it in a heartbeat. She placed a hand over her stomach, feeling sickened at the knowledge.

But Rebecca hadn't said a word.

In fact, she seemed to go to lengths to not mention it at all. And now Arabella felt like the most horrible person in the world. Complaining about getting back to her champagne-quaffing associates when Rebecca was going through serious mental anguish. Stranded in Portugal away from her dying mother, a mother who apparently wasn't due to last the night two weeks ago.

Royal Victoria, Arabella mused. She knew where it was. And she still had the lens cap. She'd pop in, give the cap back, and offer Rebecca her sympathies.

That way she wouldn't feel like such a monster. It was self-ish, but she wanted to alleviate some of her guilt.

CHAPTER 17

ARABELLA HAD ALWAYS WONDERED how some ideas could go from great to terrible in a matter of seconds.

Seeing Rebecca had seemed like a great idea on the way to the hospital. Even when she was parking the car and then entering the main entrance, she'd felt good about her decision.

She'd roamed the hospital corridors for ten minutes, looking for the cancer wards. All the while she'd been assured of her plan. It had never crossed her mind that she might be doing the wrong thing.

But the moment she overheard Rebecca's voice through an open doorway to a hospital room, she'd wondered what the hell she was thinking.

She stood awkwardly outside, now adding eavesdropping to her list of crimes, and realised how stupid she was being.

Rebecca didn't want to see her, she meant nothing to the girl. Rebecca had most likely been ecstatic to get rid of her after the journey from hell. Being forced to share a car with, and financially rely upon, a woman who must have seemed like an absolute monster.

And now she'd effectively stalked her. Photographing her driver's licence, going to her house, speaking to her neighbour, and now roaming hospital hallways. For what? A camera lens that probably cost less than five pounds.

It had been an excuse, and she knew it.

She just needed to escape her own life for a while. Because she couldn't cope with her privileged lifestyle. Because champagne gave her a headache and her millionaire fiancé was being problematic.

So, she wanted to see Rebecca. She wanted to revisit the recent times where she didn't have to think about her own problems. Times where she could freely joke and not worry about what the future would bring.

And that was how she found herself clutching a lens cap, standing in a hospital corridor, eavesdropping on Rebecca's hushed voice. Wondering what the hell she'd been thinking, and wondering if she could get out without being seen.

She started to turn around and saw a nurse looking at her with a curious expression. To escape, she'd need to walk right past her. There would no doubt be questions. She wondered if she could be arrested for entering the hospital without good reason. She wasn't eager to find out.

There was little choice, she had to go into the room. She swallowed. She'd have to style it out, walk in with confidence like she was doing something natural. Something that anyone else would have done.

She took a couple of steps and crossed the threshold. The room was dim. The harsh ceiling lighting was off, and a couple of smaller lamps gave a softer light. Rebecca sat in an upholstered chair, her legs under her, a warm drink in her hands.

The older woman from the photographs in Rebecca's wallet sat in the bed. She was propped up with cushions. She looked extremely pale and thin, but she smiled the same smile. A number of wires slipped from under the bedding and into a variety of machines lined up by the bed.

The bedside table held countless cards and flowers. A couple of miniature Christmas trees and poinsettias were included in the mix.

Arabella realised she had been there a few seconds and needed to announce her presence before the situation got even weirder. She tapped on the open door with her knuckle. Both women looked at her.

She looked apologetically to Rebecca. "I'm sorry, I—"

"Oh, is this Lucy?" Allison asked excitedly. She looked groggily from Arabella to Rebecca a few times. "See? I told you she'd make it. Everyone comes home at Christmas."

Lucy? Arabella wondered. *Who's Lucy?*

Rebecca quickly got to her feet, placing her mug on a side table. She looked panicked and raced to stand beside Arabella.

"Um, yeah, yeah, this is…" Rebecca stared at Arabella meaningfully. "This is Lucy."

Arabella instantly knew that saying she wasn't Lucy would result in immediate and painful loss of life.

She looked at Allison. "Yes, I'm Lucy. Nice to meet you, Mrs Edwards."

"Mum, I just need Lucy's help with something, I'll be back in a second," Rebecca said.

Arabella felt herself being dragged out of the room, something she knew she fully deserved. She struggled to keep up and not trip over her crutch.

Rebecca dragged them across the corridor and into an empty office. She slammed the door behind them.

"What the hell?" Rebecca demanded.

"I'm so sorry," Arabella said quickly.

"How? *How* are you here?"

Arabella picked the lens cap out of her bag and held it up. "You dropped this, I thought you might need it."

Rebecca stepped into her personal space and stared coldly at her. "Do you have some kind of tracking device on me? Did you microchip me? How are you here, Arabella?"

"I saw your driver's licence, I went to the address and the neighbour said you'd be here."

"Fucking Steve." Rebecca shook her head. She plucked the lens cap out of Arabella's hand. She took a step back and raked her fingers through her hair. "You're really telling me you left your party to deliver this? After telling me multiple times that the world would probably end if you didn't get to your party in time?"

"Who's Lucy?"

Rebecca nearly growled. "None of your business."

Arabella raised an eyebrow. "Well, as I am Lucy, I think it is my business."

"You need to leave. Now."

"Won't your mum wonder where Lucy has gone?"

"Are you enjoying this?" Rebecca asked in exasperation.

Arabella paused for a second. She'd slipped right back into bantering with Rebecca without a thought as to the serious situation they were in.

"No, I'm sorry. That was uncalled for. I... I don't know why

I came. I had to get away from the party, and I found the lens cap and wanted to return it. I didn't stop to think about how inappropriate it might be until I actually got here. I'm sorry, I know this is really strange. I don't have an agenda, I just genuinely wanted to return your property."

Rebecca leaned back against a desk, her arms folded over her chest. She looked at her feet and let out a sigh.

"I'm sorry about your mum," Arabella said. "Really. I realise now how selfish I must have sounded during the trip."

"Thank you," Rebecca said after a few moments of silence. "It wasn't that I didn't trust you. I just... didn't want to talk about it. You know what I mean?"

"Not particularly," Arabella admitted. "I'm lucky enough to never have been in such a situation."

Rebecca slowly nodded her head, still not making eye contact with Arabella.

"Lucy is the name of the girlfriend I made up. My mum, she worries about me, you know?" Rebecca mumbled as she looked up. Her eyes were red and her cheeks tearstained.

Arabella wasn't sure what to say. She opened her mouth, and then closed it again. The last thing she wanted to do now was say the wrong thing and ruin the tentative truce that had formed between them.

"I had a breakup," Rebecca confessed. "A really bad one. My mum was worried about me, and then she got sick again. So, I made up *Lucy*. I just wanted to tell her that I'd be okay, that I had someone who would be there for me and look after me when she couldn't be here anymore. It helps her."

Arabella slowly nodded. "So, she's never met Lucy?"

"No, there was always a good excuse. And Mum has been pretty sick, so she doesn't always remember stuff. I feel bad for lying to her. It is for her. I want her to know that it's okay to let go. Know that I'll be okay."

A thick silence filled the air.

"I'm sorry that I got involved," Arabella said.

"It's okay," Rebecca said. "At least now she's seen Lucy. I'll just tell her you had to go again. Mum is pretty out of it, the nurses say that it won't be much longer. They were surprised that she's lasted this long."

Arabella couldn't believe they were having such an honest and heart-breaking conversation. As if they were talking about a breakfast order. She'd never been good at emotional conversations. She never knew what to say. She often wondered if she should say anything at all.

"Are you here on your own?" Arabella finally asked.

Rebecca frowned in confusion. She slowly nodded.

"Would you like me to stay?"

Rebecca looked stunned. For the first time in the short time she had known her, Arabella saw Rebecca lost for words.

"I don't mind," Arabella added.

"Why would you do that? What about your party? And what about Alastair?"

Arabella just shrugged her shoulders. Suddenly everything seemed so insignificant. So pointless.

The very idea of returning to her party and drinking champagne and discussing business deals seemed ludicrous. How could she possibly return to that knowing that Rebecca was alone in hospital with her dying mother?

"I have nowhere else to be," Arabella said. "If you'd like the company, then I'll stay. I don't wish to intrude more so than I have already. But I don't like the idea of you being here on your own. I'm happy to pretend to be Lucy. I just think some company might be a good idea?"

Rebecca shook her head. "I can't ask you to do that."

"You're not asking, I'm offering."

Arabella realised that she *wanted* to stay. Even though it felt like it might just be the hardest thing she'd ever done. She'd mercifully never spent much time in hospital. Her health and that of her family had always been good. Heart-wrenching hospital scenes had been nothing more than on-screen entertainment.

She shivered slightly at the thought of spending time in a hospital room, visiting someone she didn't even know. Part of her wanted to take the opportunity not afforded to everyone else in the building and leave.

After all, who willingly chose to spend Christmas Eve in hospital?

But the bigger part of her wanted to stay. For the first time in a long time, Arabella was thinking about someone else other than herself. It felt good, but it also felt terrifying.

"What have you told your mum about Lucy?" Arabella asked.

Rebecca's eyes scanned her face, looking for any hint of a lie. She tugged her sweater sleeve down and rubbed the wetness from her cheeks.

"Not a lot, not anything important anyway. I just mentioned dates we'd been on. Stuff like that. But you don't have to do that, I don't want you to have to do that—"

"It's my fault. If I hadn't barged in, it wouldn't have happened. And if I just left now, then surely that would look odd?"

Rebecca slowly nodded. "Yeah, I suppose it would. It just feels so weird."

Arabella snorted a laugh.

"It is weird," she assured. "But it's been weird ever since I met you."

A grin started to form in Rebecca's face. "I suppose it has," she agreed.

"So, tell me what I need to know."

CHAPTER 18

It seemed insane. But then, lately, everything seemed insane. Over the last few years, Rebecca's life had been turned upside down.

She would never forget the terrible moment when her mother told her the news of her cancer diagnosis. It took weeks for the news to properly settle in Rebecca's mind. During that time, she just went through the motions. She was as strong as she could be and did whatever needed to be done.

Eventually, she understood and accepted that her mum was fighting a horrible and invisible illness. And for a brief while, it made her stronger. But her real strength came from a listless state where she ignored the reality of what was happening. She lived in a place where a fake smile was her best friend.

She wasn't denying the truth of what was happening. She'd accepted it and decided to push it to one side.

The news of remission wasn't as joyful as Rebecca had imagined it would be. In the back of her mind, she had always wondered if it would ever *really* be over. She celebrated and made fanciful plans with her mum for the future, but she knew they'd never really come to pass.

When the cancer came back, it was stronger than ever, shocking Rebecca with the ferocity with which it dissolved her mother's personality right before her eyes.

But Rebecca had made her mother a promise, to never let cancer win. The first day that she sat Rebecca down and told her the news, she had pleaded with Rebecca not to become sad, not to let the cancer define her.

And Rebecca tried her best. Every time she started to feel sad, she would think of the good times. Knowing that soon her mother would be gone, and she would have a choice between remembering the good times or remembering the end.

It wasn't easy, but Rebecca had luckily inherited her mother's positive personality.

Her mother didn't want to talk about her illness, but she had little else to say. And so, Rebecca had become the focus of conversation, her job, her life, her relationships.

Endless questions about finding someone new had caused Rebecca to create Lucy. Lucy embodied reassurance that Rebecca wouldn't be alone.

It was a lie, but a kind one. One that Rebecca could happily live with.

Now she hoped that Arabella would be able to keep the lie alive.

"Mum?" Rebecca whispered softly.

Her mum slowly opened her eyes. The beginnings of a smile curled on her lips. "Is it still Christmas?"

Rebecca smiled and nodded. "Yeah, you didn't think I'd let you sleep through Christmas, did you?"

A glimmer of a memory shone in her mother's eyes. "Did I… was Lucy here?"

Rebecca took a step to the side, she turned and looked Arabella. She prayed that Arabella would be able to carry off a decent performance.

Arabella took a small step forward and smiled. She looked scared.

"Hello, Mrs Edwards," Arabella said.

"Please, call me Allison. It's so nice to finally meet you. Rebecca speaks about you all the time. And I must apologise for the way I look."

Rebecca opened her mouth to speak, but before she got the chance Arabella replied, "There's nothing to apologise for."

"Look at you both, standing over me. Pull up a chair," her mum insisted.

Rebecca dragged the chair that she had been in earlier and positioned it by the bed. She gestured for Arabella to sit down. She crossed the room and retrieved the other chair from the corner and placed it beside Arabella's.

"Did you do something to your leg?"

Arabella balanced her crutch against the side of the chair, using the opportunity to give Rebecca a questioning sideways glance.

"She slipped," Rebecca said. "Nothing serious, you know what doctors are like."

Her mum laughed. "That I do," she agreed.

"I'm very sorry, Lucy, but I can't seem to remember what it is you do for a living?"

"She works in an estate agency, remember, Mum?" Rebecca said, knowing that her mum could hardly retain any information these days. The exhaustion had set in, and nowadays they just had the same conversations over and over again.

She had thought it was bad before she went to Portugal, but little did she know that was merely a taster of what was to come. She wished she had never left. Not that it mattered now.

"Oh yes, I remember now." She closed her eyes for a moment.

Rebecca wondered if she would drift off to sleep, but her eyes fluttered open again. She looked at Arabella and smiled.

"So, do you get to look at people's houses?"

"Yes, it's a very good career for a nosy person. Which I am." Arabella winked.

Rebecca smiled as her mum let out a small chuckle.

"Me too, I know it's wrong, but the best part of a party is getting to have a nose around the host's house."

Arabella laughed. "Oh yes, but then you run the risk of getting caught. Part of my job is looking around, opening cupboards and wardrobes. They can't hide anything from me."

Rebecca tuned out the conversation. She leaned back in her chair, allowing the exhaustion to slowly wash over.

For the first time in a long time, she wasn't the only person looking after her mother. She hadn't realised how exhausting the process was. But now, with Arabella beside her taking the strain, she felt like she could take a few seconds to herself. Her eyes fluttered closed, and she listened to the soft tones of the two women speaking.

CHAPTER 19

"SHE'S ASLEEP," Allison said.

Arabella glanced to her side. She suspected that Rebecca had fallen asleep a while ago. She hadn't particularly noticed, in fact she'd been enjoying talking to Allison. She turned back to face the woman.

"Yes, she must be exhausted," she said. Suddenly, she wondered if Rebecca had said anything about their journey home. She'd wait to see what information Allison provided, and hopefully get a reading on what she knew.

"She is," Allison agreed. She lovingly watched her daughter. "She is very brave, I've put her through hell."

"No," Arabella disagreed. "You mustn't think like that."

"I don't." Allison let out a soft sigh. "Not really. Becky and I agreed, when all this started, that the cancer was like a third person in our relationship. It wasn't to define me, and it wasn't to define her, or us. It was just something that was there, like a bad smell. The worst thing about cancer is it takes your identity away. I'm no longer Allison Edwards, I am a cancer patient. And

I didn't want that. I wanted to make sure that I was Allison Edwards, Rebecca's mum."

Arabella nodded. She didn't really understand. She was trying her best, but even she knew that Allison was just touching the surface of such a deep topic.

"And when I go, I don't want Rebecca to still feel that the cancer hovers around her. I want her to be happy, I don't want her to remember all of this." Allison gestured around the hospital room. "I want her to remember before, and then I want her to build a new life. A happy life. I know you two haven't been seeing each other for long, but I get a good feeling about you."

Arabella swallowed nervously.

She wasn't comfortable with lying to Allison about something so important. Up until now they had just made small talk. And she had done so willingly in the knowledge that she was helping a dying woman feel more comfortable at the end of her days.

But it sounded like the conversation was about to drift into something more serious. And Arabella wasn't good at serious, heart-to-heart conversations.

She didn't want to be making promises to a dying woman, promises that she knew she could not keep. She agreed that Rebecca was as unique, special, and deserving as Allison thought she was. Rebecca did deserve Lucy, the made-up perfect girlfriend.

"Rebecca is amazing," Arabella said. "And I know that she is going to have a great life. She'll never forget you, the good times, I mean. She never talks about all this." Arabella gestured around the room. "She talks about you, but never about the third person in your relationship."

Allison looked relieved. She let out a shaky breath. She'd noticed that Allison's breathing had become more laboured since they'd been talking.

It was clear that Allison was extremely ill. Now and then her eyes would begin to close, and then open again. When they open they were brighter, more determined. She clearly didn't want to rest.

"Thank goodness," Allison whispered. "Knowing that she'll be okay, it makes it easier."

Arabella nodded.

She couldn't imagine being in Allison's position. She didn't think she could be selfless enough to care about someone else when in such terrible pain herself. But then again, maybe the end of your life brought such clarity. She hoped that it would be a long while before she had to find out.

"Are your parents still with us?" Allison asked.

"Yes, they're divorced. I don't see my mother much, but they are both alive and well."

Allison's eyes started to close again.

Arabella let out a soft breath and gently leaned back in her chair. They had been talking for a while, and now it was probably time to let Allison rest. She sat very still and looked at her hands in her lap. She hoped that if she remained quiet, Allison would start to drift off to sleep and get the rest she desperately needed.

As the silence wore on, she became aware of heavy footsteps in the corridor towards the hospital room. Footsteps that she instantly recognised.

Thankfully, Allison had fallen asleep. Arabella grabbed her crutch and carefully manoeuvred herself around Rebecca. She walked out of the room as quietly as possible, coming face-to-face with Alastair in the corridor as she did.

His eyes sparked with fury. He was still dressed in his tuxedo. In his clenched hand was his mobile phone.

"What are you doing here?" she asked through clenched teeth.

"What am *I* doing here? What are *you* doing here? Are you injured?" He looked over her body, searching for any sign of damage.

"I'm fine," Arabella reassured him.

"Fine? Then why you are in hospital? And why didn't you say anything? You suddenly disappeared, and the next thing I knew... you were here."

"I can't explain now, I'm visiting a friend. Well, a friend's mother anyway."

His face became even redder with anger. He sucked in a breath and took a step back. He stared at the ceiling and shook his head.

Arabella rolled her eyes. She'd seen his fits of anger before, and she was beyond being affected by them.

She noticed Rebecca stood in the doorway, a questioning look on her face. Arabella shook her head to indicate she was fine.

Suddenly, the shock of seeing Alastair cleared, and the question as to why she was seeing Alastair at all reared its head.

"Wait a minute, how did you know I'm here?"

Alastair lowered his head and looked at her. A sheepish expression crept onto his face.

Arabella's eyes went wide. Her gaze drifted to the clenched fist holding his mobile phone. She glared at him. She couldn't believe he had the audacity to track her, like a microchip on a puppy.

"You have some kind of tracking software, don't you? You… you, my god, Alastair! I never gave you permission to do that."

"I did it in case of emergencies, you know, in case you ended up in the hospital." He looked around the corridor as if proving his point.

"I don't care why you did it, you should have let me know. You should have asked."

"You're my wife."

Arabella took a shocked step back.

"I am *not* your wife, and we'll be talking about this," she promised. Her eyes drifted towards Rebecca. "But not now. Now, I have to be here."

Alastair turned, seeing Rebecca for the first time. He laughed and turned back to Arabella. "Her?"

Arabella held one of her crutch towards Rebecca. Rebecca took it from her. She used the other crutch to stride towards Alastair and jabbed him hard in the chest with a pointed finger from her free hand.

"I'm staying here. You are leaving, I will call you when I can."

She could feel his breath on her face, but she didn't take a step back. She stared into his eyes. She could tell he was analysing what was happening and deciding on the best course of action. She doubted he would come to the right choice.

"I'm not leaving without you," he said. "You have to come back to your father's house. People are asking about you. What do you expect me to say? That you're… suddenly best friends with some hippie child?"

"Leave now." Arabella knew that no matter how brave Alastair appeared, he was afraid of her. He'd always had trouble controlling her. It was something that Arabella secretly enjoyed. Before, she thought it was just a game of power, but now she realised that she wasn't playing a game; she was fighting to not be controlled by him.

"Don't speak, just turn around and go. Don't push me, Alastair."

He glared at her for a few seconds. He took a step back and nodded his head.

"We will talk about this later," he said in his best menacing tone.

"We will. Now, go."

He turned around and stalked away. She watched him leave, wondering what on earth she had ever seen in the man. As he rounded the final corner and disappeared from sight, she felt Rebecca's presence beside her. She turned and took the crutch from Rebecca's hand.

"Are you sure you want to stay?" Rebecca asked, her eyebrows knitted together in confusion.

"Absolutely. My thoughts haven't changed, I still think that you shouldn't be alone. And Alastair... well, his point of view is quite frankly irrelevant to me."

A small smile appeared on Rebecca's face. Arabella knew that she was making the right decision.

CHAPTER 20

REBECCA COULDN'T BELIEVE the scene she had witnessed between Alastair and Arabella. She also couldn't believe that Arabella had chosen staying with Rebecca over him.

At first, she hadn't realised how much that meant to her. Not until she thought Arabella would cave in and go with Alastair. She had stood in the doorway willing Arabella to stay but assuming she would leave. She'd never assumed that she would have any company at this moment, but now that she had it, she was reluctant to let it go.

They both stepped back into the hospital room. Arabella paused and looked up at the clock on the wall. She turned to do the same and realised that it had just past midnight.

"Merry Christmas," Arabella whispered.

Rebecca smiled. "Merry Christmas," she whispered back. She gestured to her mother. "We should let her sleep."

Arabella looked towards the bed and slowly nodded her head.

"Have you eaten yet?" Arabella asked.

"No, I came straight here."

"Is there a place to get some food? I know how much you need to eat." Arabella joked.

Rebecca smiled despite herself. "Yes, they have a canteen, it's not great…"

"Surely it's better than some of the places we stopped at?"

"Well…" Rebecca kidded.

Arabella chuckled and gestured towards the door. Rebecca took a last look at her mother before stepping out and leading Arabella towards the hospital canteen.

They walked slowly because of Arabella's leg and in silence as Rebecca didn't know what to say. She wanted to offer her thanks and gratitude, but she didn't understand why Arabella was even there. And she didn't want to say anything that might rock the boat and cause her to leave. In a very short amount of time, Arabella's presence had become practically essential to her. She no longer thought she could do it on her own.

After a few minutes, they entered the canteen. A handful of people sat at tables, others forced to spend Christmas in hospital, either family members or workers. Some Christmas decorations had been hastily put up around the room. It was a sad attempt, and Rebecca wondered if it would have looked better without the decorations at all.

They browsed the offerings on display and, eventually, both decided on sandwiches. Arabella almost asked for coffee from the bored-looking employee, until Rebecca placed a warning hand on her forearm and softly shook her head. They both decided on tea, as it was difficult to ruin.

They sat by a window that overlooked the hospital entrance and ate in silence. In no time, Rebecca had finished a sandwich, not realising how hungry she had been. She hugged the mug of tea in her hands, enjoying the warmth.

"Thank you," Rebecca said.

"Don't mention it."

"No, I have to. I really appreciate you being here."

Arabella silently folded the sandwich wrapper and moved it to one side. She pulled her mug of tea towards her, mirroring Rebecca's pose.

"May I ask why you never said anything? I mean, you're perfectly within your right to keep it to yourself. I just wonder why you never mentioned it?"

Rebecca stared into the tea. "I think I wanted to be treated normally, to not have to worry about everything happening here. I could just be normal for a few minutes, or a few hours. No one looked at me with pity, no one hesitated every time they wanted to speak, in case they said the wrong thing."

"But I did say the wrong thing," Arabella pointed out. "And you ignored me for hours as a result. And shouted at me on the ferry."

"I'm sorry about that." Rebecca adjusted the mug in her hands.

"And you let me blather on about my party…"

Rebecca looked up at Arabella, chewing her lip anxiously. "I didn't mean… I didn't want you to…"

"I know you didn't," Arabella reassured her. "I just feel a little silly. Going on about how imperative it was for me to get home. When your need was so much greater."

Rebecca shook her head. "I didn't want it to be like that."

"Like what?"

"You know… about me."

"It should be about you."

"But I don't want that. I don't want to be the girl whose mum is dying of cancer."

Arabella smiled sadly. "You're very much like your mother."

"I'll take that as a compliment."

"Do." Arabella nodded.

Rebecca took a sip of her tea. She'd been wrong, they could ruin tea. She put the mug back on the table and continued to use it as a hand warmer.

"I felt guilty," Rebecca admitted.

"About?"

"About being in Portugal. Before I left, she was okay. I mean she was still *dying*, but it wasn't as near to the end as it is now. The chance came up to go to Portugal, get a bit of extra money and make my agent happy. I went, and she started to go downhill. I shouldn't have left."

"You couldn't have known that would happen. If you'd known, would you have stayed?"

"Of course."

"There you go then. You can't judge yourself on the unknowns," Arabella said matter-of-factly.

Rebecca clamped her lips together to prevent from chuckling out loud. Arabella had such a black-and-white view on the world.

"You know it could happen any day now," Rebecca said. "I mean she could, you know."

"Yes, I had assumed." Arabella looked down into her tea mug.

"And you're, you're okay with that?" Rebecca asked.

"Well, I'm prepared for it," Arabella said.

Rebecca watched as the older woman became lost in thought, staring into the milky tea. She couldn't understand why someone so desperate to get home to a Christmas party would suddenly abandon it to spend time with her.

Arabella was a mystery. One moment kind, another moment… not so kind. Now she was demonstrating the utmost kindness.

"I don't get it," Rebecca admitted.

Arabella's eyes met Rebecca's. "Get what?"

"You. Being here."

"I'm not sure I do either," she confessed. "But I am."

Rebecca picked up her mug and quickly gulped it down. "There's a visitors' room, it's nothing much. It has some sofas, and it's where I normally sleep when I stay the night here. I don't stay in Mum's room, I like to let her sleep. When she rests, she is not in pain."

Arabella sipped her tea. "Okay, that sounds like a good idea."

Rebecca blinked, not sure if Arabella was understanding what she was saying.

"I mean, I'm going to try to get some sleep," Rebecca clarified.

Arabella nodded. "Yes, I agreed that it's a good idea."

"So, you'll be heading home?"

"No. I'll be staying with you, if you want me to, that is? You said sofas, so I assume there's room for both of us?"

Rebecca wanted to say yes. She desperately wanted to say yes. The visitors' room, while appreciated, was lonely, dark, and scary. But it was no place for Arabella to stay. Arabella and her posh luggage. Arabella and her posh party dress.

She knew it was time to let Arabella off the hook.

"It's fine, I'll be okay," Rebecca said. "I appreciate what

you're doing, but I'm okay on my own. You go back to your party, or back home. Whatever."

Arabella regarded her carefully, her eyes never wavering as they took in Rebecca. Rebecca had a feeling that she was being analysed, that her every thought was being read.

"No, I'll stay," Arabella said finally. "I said I would, and I think you want me to."

Rebecca stuttered for a second. "I… it's… I mean…" She trailed off, after realising she had nothing to say.

She did want Arabella to stay. She didn't understand how Arabella had suddenly become her support network. The idea of going through the next few hours alone was something she dreaded.

"So, it's decided then," Arabella said. She finished her tea, grabbed her crutch, and got to her feet. "Lead the way to this visitors' room, I can see by the look in your eyes that it isn't exactly the Hilton. But as long as it doesn't have creepy porcelain dolls staring at me while I sleep, it will be a step up in the world compared to last night."

"Wow, was that only last night?"

Arabella looked down at Rebecca and nodded her head. "Yes, it's hard to believe that twenty-four hours ago we were in a creepy French château. Wondering whether the husband even existed."

Rebecca laughed. She stood up and gathered their empty mugs. "I'm sure he was just busy, or shy."

"Yeah, sure he was," Arabella muttered with a sly smile.

CHAPTER 21

THE VISITORS' room was just as dire as Arabella expected it to be. It had no windows and was lit by dim lamps that appeared to have been donated to the hospital directly after the War.

Three uncomfortable-looking sofas, two ugly armchairs, and a stack of blue rubber-coated mattresses filled the room. A door led to an en-suite bathroom.

Arabella wondered, not for the first time, or even the tenth time, what exactly she was doing. She wanted to stay, that much was obvious to her. But *why* she wished to stay still wasn't entirely clear.

Rebecca stood in the middle of the room, her hands tucked into her jeans pockets. She looked around the room apologetically.

"So, this is it," Rebecca said. "As I said, it's not much. But it's better than sleeping in the chair in Mum's room."

Arabella placed her bag on an armchair and sat on the edge of one of the sofas. She balanced her crutch on the wall beside her and started to remove her shoes. Rebecca walked over to a cupboard and open the door to reveal some sheets and pillows.

"It just sucks that it's happening at this time of year, you know?" Rebecca said. "Mum has always loved Christmas. It's always been her favourite time of year. We had so many traditions, things we'd always do. I know lots of families do; I suppose that's what makes Christmas what it is."

Arabella's family had never really had Christmas traditions. At least not anything that would find its way into a cute holiday movie. She took the offered pillow and sheet from Rebecca and made herself comfortable on her temporary bed.

"We always have mince pies. And Christmas cake. We eat far too much food," Rebecca said. "Not that we'll be doing any of that this year."

Arabella remained silent. She got the impression that Rebecca very rarely spoke about what was happening. Arabella would let her speak. Partly because she knew Rebecca needed; to get it all out. And partly because she had no idea what else to say.

She was still discovering how little she knew about Rebecca, how she had no idea how to comfort the girl. But, for some reason, Rebecca seemed to appreciate her presence. As long as that was the case, Arabella would stay.

"Mum's not really got much of an appetite at the moment," Rebecca explained. "I know she'd want me to have a normal Christmas. I don't think I can."

"I think you have to do what's right for you," Arabella said. "I know you're trying to do what's right for your mum, and that's important. But you have to look after yourself as well."

"That's what Mum keeps saying," Rebecca said.

Rebecca turned around and started making up a bed on the

sofa opposite Arabella. Arabella watched as she quickly laid the sheet down, tucking it into each corner as if she had done a hundred times before. Rebecca sat down, removed her boots, and stretched on the sofa, reaching her arms above her.

Arabella watched, unable to drag her eyes away from Rebecca. She wanted to help, but she had no idea how. She could see that the girl was tense, ready to leap into action at a moment's notice. She couldn't blame her, but she knew Rebecca had to rest.

The worst was yet to come.

"Get some sleep," Arabella instructed.

Rebecca looked at her and let out a sigh. "I don't think I'll be able to," she admitted.

Arabella could see the exhaustion in Rebecca's face. She knew that the girl would fall asleep within seconds once she permitted herself to.

Arabella adjusted her sheeting and pillow and laid herself down. In a million years she never would have thought that she would be spending Christmas Eve on a second-hand sofa in a hospital waiting room. With a woman she barely knew.

Maybe it was the feeling of doing something for someone else, of doing something charitable, but it felt like the right thing to do.

"Just close your eyes," Arabella said softly. "Think of all those things about Christmas that you love." She sighed dramatically. "All those sugary treats, pies, and cakes, ridiculous paper hats, and whatever other ludicrous traditions that you hold so dear."

Rebecca snorted a laugh.

Arabella smiled. She turned her head, seeing that Rebecca was still staring up at the ceiling.

"I'm pretty sure I just told you to close your eyes."

Rebecca turned to regard her and slowly nodded her head. Her eyes fluttered closed.

"It's Christmas Day, so imagine that Father Christmas—"

"Santa," Rebecca corrected.

Arabella chuckled. "Very well, Santa, is making his way around the world delivering presents all the good boys and girls. Is that not how it goes?"

"Something like that," Rebecca agreed.

"Eating one hundred metric tons of Christmas treats and drinking gallons of milk or brandy, depending on the property value of the house he is visiting."

"This bedtime story is a little different to what I remember from being a kid," Rebecca said with a laugh.

"Well, it's the one you're getting. Now, stop interrupting. I'm pretty sure that there is something about reindeer."

CHAPTER 22

Distant noises began to invade the quiet space, but Rebecca was used to it. The sounds of the nurses beginning their day, usually at an ungodly hour, had become her new alarm clock. She turned to lay on her back. She opened her eyes and stared at the ceiling.

Another day, she told herself. *Christmas Day.*

As she started to remember the events of the previous day, her head snapped around to look at the other sofa.

She winced.

Arabella was gone. Folded sheets sat atop a pillow on the arm of the sofa.

She blew out a breath. She couldn't blame the woman. At least she had waited until she had gone to sleep.

She looked at her watch. Her eyebrows rose in shock, it was already nine! She couldn't believe she had slept so long. She hadn't had a full night of sleep for weeks. She quickly felt guilty, her mum would have been woken that morning by a nurse.

She sat up and ran her fingers through her hair and rubbed

her face. She pulled on her boots, stood up, and gathered the linens from her bed. She rolled them into a ball and threw them on top of Arabella's neatly folded sheets. She'd deal with them later. Right now, she had to pretend to enjoy what was bound to be the worst Christmas of her life.

She put her hand on the door handle and paused while she took a deep breath. Once she had exhaled, she put a smile on her face and walked out of the room.

She turned the corner and walked the few steps up the corridor towards her mother's room. The moment she crossed the threshold, she froze. Her jaw dropped, and she stared at the room in shock.

"Morning, darling, Merry Christmas," her mum said.

Rebecca tore her eyes away from the rest of the room and looked at her mother. She was so stunned she couldn't form any words.

"Isn't it amazing? It was all Lucy, you know."

"L-Lucy?" Rebecca stammered.

She looked around the room, tinsel and brightly coloured paper decorations had been hung. A tacky blow-up Christmas tree, complete with integrated hanging decorations, sat in pride of place on the table in front of the window. Another table was filled with Christmas treats, mince pies, Christmas cake, cookies, and lots more. A bottle of champagne, and what looked like non-alcoholic wine, sat on the bedside table beside some crystal-cut champagne flutes.

"Yes, she bought too much tinsel so her and Abigail, you know the new morning nurse, have gone to share the wealth with the main ward."

Rebecca looked to her mother. She was sat up in bed, a paper hat on her head. In her lap, a box of her favourite

Christmas chocolates. And, much to Rebecca's amazement and relief, she seemed to have eaten a few.

It almost looked normal. If you could ignore the hospital bed and equipment, it could nearly be a real Christmas. Rebecca felt tears start to flood her eyes and quickly turned away. Crying was not allowed. She knew that once she started, she wouldn't stop.

"We thought we'd let you sleep in," her mum said. "Get some rest after your long trip."

Rebecca pretended to analyse the blow-up Christmas tree, she smiled at the very thought of Arabella puffing out her cheeks, blowing up the hideous, tacky decoration.

"Thank you," Rebecca said.

"She cares about you," her mum said. "A lot."

Rebecca didn't answer. She didn't know what to say. Maybe Arabella did care about her, maybe it was some kind of guilt. At this point she didn't know. And that probably wasn't going to change in the near future either.

"Ah, you're up."

Rebecca turned around to see Arabella walking into the room. A chuckle escaped Rebecca's lips as she noted the paper hat on her head.

"One word about what is on top of my head, and you will regret it," Arabella said with a smirk.

Rebecca held up her hands. "Wouldn't dream of it," she replied, but she was unable to keep the smile off her face.

"I was worried you'd sleep away Christmas," Arabella gently chided.

Rebecca noticed Arabella looking towards her mother with a frown. Arabella walked over to the side of the bed and took the box of chocolates away from the sleeping woman.

"She's been drifting in and out all morning," she explained. She placed the chocolates on the bedside table. Then she picked up a mince pie and held out towards Rebecca. "Breakfast?"

"When did you do all this?" Rebecca took the mince pie and started to peel the foil tray away from the delicious pastry goodness.

"I woke up early, I thought I might as well get a start on making Christmas. I may not have a white fluffy beard and wear a red suit, but I thought I'd do."

"You do," Rebecca whispered. "Thank you for this, it's... incredible."

"Well, it's only just started," Arabella said.

"Shouldn't you be getting home? Aren't they going to miss you?"

Rebecca really didn't want to bring it up. She didn't want Arabella to go, but she also didn't want Arabella to feel obligated to stay. Because surely that could be the only reason that she was staying?

"I keep telling you, I'm staying," Arabella said. "Now, come on, I have something for you."

"For me?" Rebecca frowned.

"Yes, for you. Come on." Arabella turned on her crutch and walked out of the room. Rebecca quickly followed her, surprised at the speed with which Arabella could move when she wanted to.

They walked down the corridor and back towards the visitors' room. Rebecca wondered what else Arabella had up her sleeve.

Arabella opened the door and walked in. She paused in the middle of the room and nodding her head towards a wrapped Christmas present on Rebecca's sofa. Rebecca stared at the present. She hadn't even thought of getting or giving any presents this year. Seeing a Christmas present beautifully wrapped, with ribbons and a bow, took her by surprise.

"Don't just stare at it," Arabella said. She placed her crutch next to her sofa and sat down.

"You got me a present?" Rebecca asked.

"Well, the evidence would indicate that that is the case, wouldn't it?" Arabella rolled her eyes.

"Why did you get me a present?"

"Because it's Christmas," Arabella replied. "Are you going to open it or not?"

Rebecca sat tentatively next to the box.

"I promise it's not a porcelain doll."

Rebecca chuckled. She gently picked it up and placed it on her lap. She found the ends of the ribbon and delicately pulled. She felt like such a fraud, ordinarily she would have ripped the parcel open in seconds. But in Arabella's presence, with the older woman still dressed to the nines from her Christmas Eve party, Rebecca acted with a decorum she never knew she had.

After carefully removing the ribbon, she searched for where the paper had been taped down and began to slowly pick at the tape.

"We'll be here all day if that's how you open gifts," Arabella commented.

"Shush you."

Rebecca sped up slightly, starting to rip the paper. Excitement was building within her, but she tried to keep it down. After all, it was quite likely that Arabella had bought her a joke gift. She removed the wrapping paper and put it to one side. A plain cardboard box sat in her lap.

"I put it in that box, so it would be easier to wrap," Arabella explained.

Rebecca open the top of the box. She peered inside and saw a label. Her eyes widened in surprise. She reached her hand into the box and pulled out the contents. The box dropped to her feet, and she stared at the Manfrotto backpack.

"It's better than that tatty old rucksack you have," Arabella said. "You wouldn't want to damage your camera."

Rebecca turned the camera bag over in her hands, examining it from all angles. It was perfect. It would perfectly contain all of her travel things, with a safe space for her camera, lenses, and equipment. She knew because she had longingly stared at it in a shop window for a number of months. The hefty price tag always made it an impossible purchase.

"I can't accept this, I know what this cost," Rebecca said. She looked up at Arabella. "How did you even manage to get it?"

Arabella spread her hands in obvious gesture. "This is London. You can get anything at any time."

"It's incredibly generous, too generous. I'm sorry I can't accept it."

"You can accept it, and you will. In the not-too-distant future the handle on your rucksack will snap and your camera, and your livelihood, will be broken. Besides, it's Christmas."

"I didn't get you anything." Rebecca stared back down at the bag. Her fingers ran over the logo.

"You're sharing Christmas with me. And let's not forget, you drove me home from Faro."

Rebecca laughed. "You paid for the car," she reminded Arabella.

"I had no idea how argumentative you could be," Arabella

said. "I might just complain to your mother. Accept the damn bag."

Rebecca gripped the bag lovingly and bit her lip. Arabella was right, her rucksack was dangerously in need of repair. It wouldn't be long before it broke, she'd been lucky that it hadn't broken and damaged her camera equipment already.

"Thank you, really, thank you… for everything. I don't know how you did this, but I really appreciate it."

Arabella smiled. "Well, when you get up at a reasonable time and set your mind to something, you can get a hell of a lot done."

"So I see!" She hugged her bag to her chest. It smelt of future adventures.

"I arranged for a Christmas dinner to be delivered to the ward. Yes, I spoke with the head nurse first. I imagine whatever they had planned to serve would have been… shall we say, less than desirable? Anyway, it's on the way and hopefully we can convince your mother to have a couple of bites."

Rebecca blinked. "Y-you arranged for Christmas dinner to be delivered to the entire ward?"

Arabella grabbed her crutch and pushed herself off the sofa to stand. "Yes, as I said, when you get up at a reasonable time you can get a hell of a lot done."

"Did you get any sleep?" Rebecca asked.

"Some." Arabella nodded. "But, to be honest, sleep escapes me at the moment."

Rebecca assumed as much. Arabella did seem to be a woman escaping from something. She'd watched the interaction between Arabella and Alastair with great interest. Of course, she had never made her dislike of the man a secret. And she had to admit she had been secretly pleased to see them argue, especially to see Arabella stand up for herself. She knew Arabella could do better. Much better.

"I'm sorry to hear that," Rebecca said.

Arabella shrugged. "It is what it is. But at least that means I get to spend Christmas here, as long as you'll still have me?"

"Absolutely, you're like my very own little Santa," she joked.

Arabella rolled her eyes. "Careful, I could still go home, you know."

"Please don't," tumbled from Rebecca's lips before she had time to stop it. "I mean, if you still want to stay, I'd still like you to be here."

Arabella looked down at her kindly. "I still want to stay."

Rebecca chuckled bitterly. "I honestly can't think why, but I'm glad you're here."

"I know things are grim. But no matter what happens, your mum smiled this morning. She ate some Christmas chocolates, and, for a couple of moments, things seemed normal. That's what you need to hold onto."

Rebecca put her bag to the side and stood up. "You're right. Let's go and be festive."

CHAPTER 23

ARABELLA STOOD outside the hospital's main entrance. She pulled the jacket she had borrowed from Rebecca around her shoulders.

Snow had been falling steadily for the last few hours. She looked out at the snow-covered car park in front of her. Any other day it would have been a beautiful sight, a perfect wintry Christmas scene. But this wasn't any other day; this was the day that Rebecca had lost her mother.

It happened so fast. One moment they were eating Christmas dinner, drinking the non-alcoholic wine, reminiscing about Christmases gone by. The next Allison's eyes had started to flutter closed. A few moments later, she opened her eyes and started to look around in confusion. Something had clearly been wrong. Rebecca rushed to get a nurse.

By the time the nurse arrived, Allison had closed her eyes again and drifted off into an endless sleep.

Arabella hadn't known what to do. She'd never been in that kind of situation before, she didn't know how to act or what to say. She stood uselessly in the room, watching as Rebecca flopped into a chair and stared helplessly at her mother.

They remained like that for ten long and agonising minutes. The low sound of Christmas music continued to stream through Arabella's phone. It seemed utterly surreal.

The head nurse had entered the room and started speaking to Rebecca in hushed tones. Arabella had taken the opportunity to get some fresh air. Remembering that she was still wearing a thin party dress and knowing that snow had been falling thick and fast, she had grabbed Rebecca's jacket.

She had hoped that the fresh air would give her a sense of clarity. That things would seem better, that she would be able to figure out what to do next.

Sadly, it was too much to ask of fresh air. She felt just as confused, lost, and helpless as she had inside the hospital.

She felt guilty. She worried that she had overexcited Allison, that her desire to create a perfect Christmas had resulted in the woman's premature death. The nurse had explained she could have passed at any point within the last few days. And that it was just bad luck that it happened to be Christmas Day.

Arabella hoped that was true. She certainly hoped that Rebecca would see it that way. She wondered why on earth she had stayed. Had she just ended up making things worse?

The automatic doors slid open. Arabella looked up to see Rebecca step outside. Rebecca rubbed her arms in protest at the chilly air, she wore jeans and a thin sweater.

Arabella immediately started to remove the jacket from her shoulders, but Rebecca held her hand up.

"It's okay," Rebecca reassured her.

Arabella paused. "Are you sure? It's freezing out here."

"I'm sure." Rebecca rubbed her hands together. She stood beside Arabella, leaning on the wall.

"I don't know what to do," Rebecca admitted softly.

"What do you mean?"

"I have all this paperwork to fill in, and I should probably go home. But I don't want to. I feel like I should stay here. It's so weird to try to understand that I don't need to be here anymore. And I don't want to be home either. I feel... untethered."

Rebecca stared out at the white blanket of snow, lost in thought.

"Rebecca, I'm *so* sorry," Arabella said.

She slowly turned to regard Arabella, a frown on her face. "Why?"

"I shouldn't have done so much, it was all just too much. I wanted to make a perfect Christmas. Clearly, it taxed your mother."

Rebecca shook her head. "No, no, don't think this was your fault. It's amazing that she even got to *see* Christmas Day. She's had good days and bad days for the last few weeks. There's been many times when I thought I'd lose her. The fact that she got to see Christmas Day, and that you made it so amazing, means more to me than I can ever say."

Arabella looked into Rebecca's eyes, unable to detect a hint of a lie.

"I will never be able to thank you enough for what you did today. I think today was the first day in a long time that Mum forgot that she was ill. She had fun, she had a great day. If I could... if I could *choose* which day would be her last day, then it would probably be this day."

Arabella felt relief. All she wanted to do was help. The

thought that maybe she had caused irreparable damage had been too much to bear.

She looked at her watch, it was six o'clock in the evening. She hadn't heard from any of her family all day. Alastair had clearly said something to prevent them from getting in touch. She didn't feel like going home either.

"Let's go somewhere," Arabella suggested.

Rebecca looked at her in confusion. "Like where?"

"I don't know. Let's go somewhere, see something. Away from here."

Rebecca turned and gazed out at the heavy snow falling on top of cars. She looked so lost. Arabella's heart clenched at the sight.

"You know, when my grandmother died… I went to the cinema," Arabella said.

A disbelieving smile crossed Rebecca's face.

"The cinema?"

"Yes. I went with my two cousins," Arabella explained. "And we went to see some children's movie; we were all in our late teens. It was two-fifteen on a Tuesday. We heard she'd died and just had no idea what to do. Everything seemed so strange. She'd been ill and in hospital for a while. It was just a matter of time until she died. I think we'd all grieved her for a long time before she died."

Arabella took a few steps forward, leaving the safety of the canopy and now stood directly in the snow. She held out her hand and watched as snowflakes began to land and dissolve in her palm.

"We didn't want to eat, didn't want to stay home. We didn't know what to do. Nobody ever really explains to you what to do when somebody dies. Especially if you've been mourning that person for some time. You're not going to burst into tears, throw yourself on top of your bed, and be inconsolable for a few hours. And yet you're not just going to get on with your life either."

Arabella watched as the snowflakes melted. She let out a sigh. She lowered her hand and turned back to face Rebecca.

"And so, we did something utterly bizarre, and went to the cinema. We bought tickets to the only thing that was playing at that time of day. We walked in and doubled the audience. And all six of us watched some mind-numbing children's film, I couldn't tell you what it was even about now."

Arabella chuckled and shook her head. "At one point, my younger cousin leaned close to me and whispered in my ear that our grandmother just died a few hours before, and now we were at the cinema, and how weird it felt. And I agreed with her, but neither of us could think of a single other thing to do."

Rebecca slowly nodded her head. "I understand what you mean, I'm not ready to grieve. I've been grieving on and off for months. And, as much as I hate myself for thinking this, there is a small part of me that is relieved that she is no longer in pain."

She started to cry. Arabella rushed forward and pulled her into a one-armed hug.

"It's going to be okay, we're going to get through the rest of this day together," Arabella promised.

Rebecca sniffed and nodded her head against Arabella's shoulder.

"I just don't know what to do," she mumbled.

"And that's okay. There's no rule book for these situations. Don't be so hard on yourself."

Arabella tightened her arm around Rebecca, grasping her

crutch in her other hand. Soft sobs shook the younger woman, and Arabella knew she'd do anything to make everything better.

"I have an idea," she said. "Do you trust me?"

"Of course," Rebecca answered without hesitation.

She paused for a moment. She didn't think she'd ever heard someone have such faith in her, especially someone she hardly knew. She swallowed and cleared the wayward thought from her mind.

"Good, then I have an idea."

CHAPTER 24

Rebecca looked around the familiar interior. A few hours ago, she would have given anything to have been out of the car. Now, she was almost relieved to be back in it. Although, she was going to have to have a word with Arabella about driving to the hospital with her foot in the cast.

She rubbed her face with the palms of her hands.

Everything seemed blank. Confusing didn't begin to cover it. She felt like she was waking up from a long, deep sleep. One where her life had been indefinitely on hold.

She didn't know what normal felt like anymore. It had been replaced a while ago. Life had been surreal for so long that she now struggled to remember the real world from the fake.

She couldn't believe that she had burst into tears on Arabella's shoulder. She knew she could be forgiven for crying, her mother just died. But it seemed like Arabella was the only thing holding her together at the moment. It wasn't fair on Arabella. Fate had thrown them together, nothing more.

The passenger door opened. Arabella bent down and poked her head in.

"Could you open the boot?"

Rebecca pulled the lever.

She noticed three hospital orderlies standing behind Arabella, all carrying boxes. Arabella directed them to put the boxes in the boot, reminding them not to damage her precious luggage that was still there.

In a matter of moments, they were done and walked back towards the hospital. Arabella slammed the boot closed and took her seat in the car.

"You *drove* here?" Rebecca chastised immediately.

"No, I flew here," Arabella replied. She pulled her seatbelt around her, clicking into place. "But, look at me, I'm wearing my seatbelt." She smiled.

Rebecca rolled her eyes and shook her head. She put her own seatbelt on.

"So, what did, um, what did they say?" Rebecca asked hesitantly.

Arabella's face turned serious. "After you said goodbye, I sat down with the head nurse and filled out the most important paperwork as best I could, based on what you told me. The rest is in one of the boxes. There is a leaflet explaining what you need to do, and someone from the hospital will call you in the next three days. All of her belongings are in the boxes."

Rebecca swallowed. "Thank you for dealing with that."

"My pleasure. I'm a lot better at dealing with paperwork than I am with people."

"You seem to be very good at dealing with people," Rebecca commented.

Arabella smiled wryly. "You wouldn't have said that two days ago."

She was right. Two days ago, Rebecca would have considered throttling Arabella without feeling much guilt at all.

"I've gotten to know you. You are a lot softer than you would have people believe."

Arabella chuckled. "I deny everything. Anyway, I have an idea about a place to go. If you're up for driving?"

"It's Christmas Day, isn't everything closed?" Rebecca asked.

"Asked by someone who has clearly never left their house on Christmas Day. The country may have ground to a halt on Christmas Day forty years ago, but not these days. Now, are you going to drive, or do I have to?"

Rebecca started the engine. "Where to, O navigator?"

CHAPTER 25

"This is freezing," Rebecca complained.

"It certainly is," Arabella agreed. "I'd offer you another drink, but you insist on driving." Arabella sipped from her plastic wineglass.

"Do I need to remind you again that Jose would not be happy with you invalidating his insurance by driving the car?"

"Jose isn't here," Arabella pointed out.

Rebecca laughed. She leaned on the handrail and looked out over the front of the boat. She regarded the pretty, twinkling lights of London. Lights that she would have been able to appreciate more if there wasn't a strong wind filled with snowflakes blowing in her face.

The idea of taking a cruise ship on the Thames had seemed like such a good idea. Right up until the moment they actually did it.

Luckily, Arabella had stopped off at her house and picked up a thick winter coat and scarf. Arabella's house was a smaller but no less impressive mansion than her father's the night before. The lights had been off. Arabella said that Alastair would probably, and hopefully, still be at her father's house.

After the short stop, they had driven towards the City, looking for something to do. Much to Rebecca's surprise, the roads were quiet but certainly not deserted.

Arabella was right, Rebecca had always assumed that everybody was indoors with their family on Christmas Day, despite knowing that London was a large and diverse city, consisting of many different cultures and religions. Somehow, she'd never stopped to think about the countless people who didn't celebrate Christmas, or those who just celebrated Christmas in a different way to herself.

As they had driven deeper into the City, the crowds had started to grow. Bars, restaurants, and shops were open. People scooped handfuls of snow from fence railings and parked cars and threw them at one another.

Seeing other people just doing their own thing helped Rebecca to not feel so alone.

Arabella had directed Rebecca to park in what was clearly a no-parking area. The older woman claimed that no parking enforcement officers would be out on Christmas Day. She also unexpectedly made a big deal of her cast and her sudden inability to walk too far.

A few moments later and they were at the dock, awaiting the cruise ship's arrival with a few other partygoers. Rebecca had asked Arabella if it was booze cruise. Arabella had chuckled, asking if she looked like the kind of person who would frequent such an event.

The second they got on the boat, Rebecca remembered why she didn't much like boats.

It wasn't that she got seasick, in fact she loved the feel of being on the water. It was the elements, in warmer climates, the sun would beat down mercilessly. In colder climates, like today, the biting wind felt ten times worse on open water.

But, despite the discomfort of the cold wind and the flakes of snow, she had to admit that she felt energised and alive. Something that she hadn't felt a couple of hours before.

Never in her wildest dreams would she ever have considered getting on a cruise ship on the Thames on Christmas Day.

"This is nice," she admitted.

Arabella blinked in surprise. "Aren't you the person who was *just* complaining about how cold it is?"

"Oh, it's cold, freezing. But this, this is nice." Rebecca pointed to the view.

Arabella leaned on the railing and smiled as she looked at the unique mix of old and new architecture.

"Yes, it is. London has always been my favourite city. Obviously, I'm biased. I live and work here. And I was born here. But there's something about London, the architecture, the people, the soul of the city."

"Aw, that's quite poetic," Rebecca said.

"Of course it is, I'm a saleswoman. It's in my blood." Arabella gestured to the buildings with her hand. "I could sell you any one of these."

Rebecca laughed. "You may be the best saleswoman there is. And you may well make me *want* to buy one. But I could never afford one."

Arabella shrugged. "That's what loans are for."

"Buying office blocks?" Rebecca asked.

"Why not?"

"Oh, I see, and what do you think I should do with this

office block you just sold me?" Rebecca asked, a smirk on her face.

"Rent it out, make a profit. Buy another, from me, of course." Arabella winked.

"Of course," Rebecca agreed. "Until I own half of London?"

"Absolutely. And then you'll have your own private yacht to take night-time tours on Christmas Day. And appreciate the view of your empire."

"I don't think I'm an office block kind of person."

Arabella looked at her with a wistful smile. "You're right. I think you need to build a portfolio of apartments instead. Residential. Not as much profit but more security."

"Do you have a portfolio of apartments?"

"A small one, yes. Not as many listings as I'd like. I've often forgone good deals to sell them to my clients. A tactical decision while building up Henley's."

"You really love it, don't you? Work, I mean. You talked about it a lot in the car, and I can see how passionate you are about it now."

Arabella looked down at the water.

"I do love it," she admitted. "But, I don't know, it's complicated."

"That's what people say when they are scared of the truth," Rebecca said.

Arabella chuckled and looked up at her. "Oh, is that so?"

"Yep." Rebecca nodded her head. "People only ever describe something as complicated when they know what they want isn't what other people want. Like, when someone is married but they want a divorce. They'll tell someone else that it's complicated. Because they know that they want a divorce, but they don't want to get a divorce because that will be messy and scary. Complicated is a great word to stop people doing something that will end up being really messy."

Arabella regarded her silently. The smile slipped from her face.

Rebecca felt dread run up her spine, colder than the icy winds bouncing up from the waters below. She wondered if she had gone too far, if her big mouth had got her into more trouble.

"I'm sorry, I shouldn't have—"

"No, no, it's fine," Arabella reassured her. She tore her eyes from Rebecca and looked down once again at the choppy waters below them. "I was just wondering why I don't have a friend in my life who is as honest as you are."

"Self-preservation?" Rebecca guessed.

Arabella grinned. "Most likely."

A waiter made his way along the deck, expertly balancing a tray of drinks. Arabella stood up and turned to face him.

"Can I have another champagne, and can my friend here have a hot chocolate?"

The waiter nodded and hurried away to get their orders.

Rebecca looked in surprise from Arabella to the departing waiter. It had been a while since someone had ordered for her. Especially ordered exactly what she wanted.

Arabella looked startled.

"If you don't want to drink it, you can hold it and get some warmth from it," she explained.

A slight blush appeared on Arabella's cheeks as she realised that she had ordered for Rebecca without asking what she wanted.

"I like hot chocolate," Rebecca said, eager to quell Arabella's embarrassment.

Arabella turned to face the water. "You're right, I am scared of the truth. I am using the word complicated as a shield of sorts. It's not complicated at all, if I'm honest with myself."

Rebecca was surprised to hear the admission. It was so softly spoken that it was nearly eaten up by the engine noise and the waves.

She took a step closer, leaning on the handrail beside Arabella and looking out at the illuminated cityscape.

She remained quiet, wishing that Arabella would speak again.

After a few moments, the woman let out a sigh. "I don't want to marry Alastair. I think I've always known that, I just didn't see any other option. He's a nice enough man. Trust me, I've dated worse. But I'm... well, I'm trapped in this engagement now. I don't expect you to understand, but my life has been mapped out for me. There are certain things I'm expected to do. And I always knew that, and I was always comfortable with that. But now the time is here, I'm scared. But it's too late to turn back now."

"It's never too late," Rebecca promised.

Arabella laughed bitterly. "Oh, it is, believe me. Everyone knows about the engagement, everyone is planning for the wedding, and what comes after. To pull out now would be such a public disaster. Not to mention that it wouldn't change anything. If I didn't marry Alastair then I'd just end up marrying someone else. Better the devil you know."

"Yeah, you're right," Rebecca agreed. "Because, like, it is the dark ages and you're totally going to be auctioned off to a man anyway, so you might as well pick this one, right? And getting married means that your life is over. You need to stay home and let the men deal with the business while you pump out babies and arrange dinner parties."

Arabella looked up at her. She raised her eyebrow.

"Ouch," she said without feeling.

"I just don't get it," Rebecca continued. "You're brilliant, you're intelligent, impressive, you're clearly an important part of the business. Why do you have to give all that up?"

"I—"

"Actually, I don't want to hear your answer," Rebecca cut her off. "Just answer me this question: do you want to? Do you want to marry someone you obviously don't love? Do you want to give up work? And, do you want to be some weird Stepford Wife?"

"That's not the point," Arabella countered.

"Yeah, it is. It's completely the point. Come on, Arabella, you just saw how short and unfair life can be. I may not know you that well, but I know you are motivated and you seem to like challenges. You must have a list of things you want to accomplish in your life? Have you done them? Or will you do them after you're married? I can't see you having a bucket list that consists of making the perfect omelette, whisking eggs into a perfect velvety scramble or whatever you have to do to make a perfect omelette. I just don't think they are the accomplishments you want to tick off, but maybe I'm wrong?"

The waiter returned. "Excuse me."

Rebecca turned around and smiled at him. "Thank you," she said as she took both of the drinks, handing the champagne to Arabella.

Arabella mumbled her gratitude and took the glass, retreating back to her view of the dark water.

"I'm sorry," Rebecca muttered.

She didn't know why she felt the need to push Arabella. It was like she had a personal mission to stop her from giving up work and, more importantly, marrying someone she didn't love.

But she didn't know why it was so important to her. She hardly knew Arabella and she was trying to fix her life.

"You don't need to apologise, you're right," Arabella confessed. "I got myself into a mess, and I need to get myself out of it. I'm not quite sure how to do that, but I will. I shan't spend the rest of my days making award-winning omelettes."

Rebecca smiled so hard it hurt her cold cheeks. She wrapped her hands tightly around the hot chocolate mug, enjoying the feeling of warmth against her cold palms.

"I should thank you," Arabella continued. She still leaned on the handrail, but now turned to focus all of her attention on Rebecca. "Seriously, you've been a pain in my side since the moment I met you, but I am so glad I met you."

"You have a funny way of saying thank you," Rebecca pointed out.

"You opened my eyes, and that's not an easy thing to do," Arabella carried on, ignoring her comment. "If I'd caught that plane and flown home as planned, I don't think I ever would have addressed that nagging feeling in the pit of my stomach. So, thank you."

Arabella took a step forward and placed a soft kiss on Rebecca's cheek.

Rebecca cursed that she had stood in the cold wind for so long that her cheek was numb. To make up for the dulled nerve endings in her cheek, she quickly inhaled the complex aroma of Arabella's perfume.

"You're welcome," Rebecca managed to say. She was relieved

when she got the words out and realised that she hadn't stuttered or squeaked. "And thank you, I couldn't have managed today without you."

"Oh, you would've been fine." Arabella returned to her place, leaning on the handrail.

Rebecca wanted to step closer but knew it was inappropriate. She was emotionally drained, as was Arabella. But Arabella was also tired and probably on her way to being drunk. And Rebecca didn't know if she just wanted some human comfort or if what she was starting to feel for Arabella was something more.

She noticed Arabella shiver slightly.

"Maybe we should head inside?" she suggested.

"We can't enjoy the view from in there," Arabella commented.

"I can," Rebecca replied with a sigh as she gazed at Arabella. "I—I mean, the windows are fine. We can... see the view through the... the windows."

Arabella was too busy deciding what to do with her glass as she looked at her crutch to catch Rebecca's rambling. Rebecca reached out and took the champagne glass from her.

"Thank you." Arabella adjusted her crutch and made her way slowly towards the door to the interior seating area.

Rebecca followed her, chastising herself for her slip.

Arabella was straight, and Rebecca didn't want to fall into the lesbian stereotype of hitting on any attractive woman with a pulse. She could just be friends with Arabella, especially as the friendship would probably only last a few more hours. Until Arabella sobered up and realised that she was hanging out with someone so far below her status. Eventually Arabella would decide that it was time to go home, and that would be the end of whatever it was they had.

Rebecca was grateful that she'd had Arabella's help and companionship as long as she had. She knew that time was running out and now she just needed to enjoy the company, build some positive memories of this terrible and messed-up Christmas Day.

CHAPTER 26

Two Weeks Later

Arabella hung up the phone. She pulled her laptop closer and typed some notes into the system.

"Helen, can you get the contract ready for Mrs Simmons? She wants to come in this afternoon to sign," she called out.

Arabella's assistant Helen entered her office. "I'll get it printed out in a moment; any idea what time she will be here?"

Arabella laughed. "As usual, she's not been helpful enough to provide a time."

Helen took some files from Arabella's out-tray and put the morning post in the in-tray. She fussed around the desk, removing screwed-up pieces of paper and picking up the three used coffee mugs.

"Make sure you take some time to have lunch today. I know it's busy, but you have to eat."

Arabella looked up at her assistant and smiled. "Thank you, I'll do my best."

"Don't think I don't recognise that tone."

"What tone?" Arabella asked.

"The one you use to appease customers," Helen pointed out. "That means you won't do whatever you say you will do."

Arabella opened a file on her desk and started to read through the papers.

"You know it's January, right? Our busiest time of year? Everyone who put their life on hold for December has suddenly woken up from their turkey-induced coma and wants everything done yesterday."

Helen let out a long-suffering sigh. She stood in front of the desk and looked impatiently at her.

"Fine, fine. I will *try* to make some time," Arabella reassured her.

She had no idea where she would find that time, though. The pile of work on her desk was growing exponentially each day. She pressed some buttons on the keyboard to print the document she was working on.

"We have to get the new keys cut for Monmouth Street," Arabella said. "I suppose I could do that on my way back from my dinner appointment with the Chinese investors."

"It's already done. They're in my desk drawer," Helen replied.

She pointed to a high stack of files that sat on the floor beside Arabella's desk. "Are those to be filed?"

Arabella glanced at them and felt a pang of guilt for letting them grow into an unmanageable mess over the past few days.

"Yes, but I'll do it," she said.

"I can do it," Helen offered.

"It's my mess, I'll clean it up later this afternoon," Arabella offered.

Helen raised an eyebrow and shook her head. It was taking a while for Helen to get used to the new Arabella. The post-Christmas Arabella.

She turned around to see why her printer hadn't sprung to life. A message regarding the toner flashed on the small screen. It wasn't a surprise, January really was a hectic month and the device had been spitting out contracts like they were going out of fashion.

She turned back to her laptop and reprinted the document in the main office instead.

"Well, if you change your mind, let me know," Helen instructed gently.

Helen was the kind of person who wouldn't take any crap from Arabella, but still knew who was boss. Arabella enjoyed working with her because she knew that Helen wouldn't hesitate to tell her off if necessary.

She leaned on the desk and pushed herself to standing. She picked up her crutch and started to make her way to the main office to get her freshly printed documents, hoping that toner was holding up better.

"I'll be fine," she reassured Helen as they left her office.

The shop was buzzing with people, and she quickly looked around to check that everything looked satisfactory. All staff members were on the phones or speaking directly with customers.

She walked to the corner and saw her documents shooting out of the top of the printer. Once the job was finished, she picked up the still-warm papers and started to check through the details one last time.

"Can I help you?" she heard the receptionist say.

"I'm here to see Arabella Henley," a familiar voice replied.

Arabella heart beat a little faster. She pretended she hadn't heard the conversation and glanced up at the glass window in front of her to check her reflection. She didn't know why it mattered to her, but she casually tamed her hair regardless.

"Miss Henley?" the receptionist asked as she approached.

"Yes?" Arabella asked, wishing she'd bothered making a note of the new girl's name. It would look better if she knew her name.

"There's a Miss Edwards here to see you."

Arabella took a calming breath before looking up and towards Rebecca. She tried to look calm and put together, but she wasn't sure she was managing it.

Rebecca stood nervously in the reception area, holding a large bouquet of flowers and waving at her. Arabella raised her hand to wave back, but, at the last minute, thought better of the geeky gesture. She turned it into a gesture for Rebecca to come and join her.

"Thank you," she said to the receptionist, giving her permission to go back to her desk.

"Well, hello there, Miss Edwards," Arabella said once Rebecca had approached her. "Lovely to see you again."

"Hi," Rebecca replied. Her eyes roamed over Arabella quickly. "You're looking good... I mean well, you're looking well."

Arabella grinned. She could cope better with her own nerves if she knew Rebecca was just as nervous.

"Thank you, you do too."

"These are for you." Rebecca gestured to the flowers.

"They're beautiful, you didn't have to do that, though."

Arabella noticed a few members of staff were starting to stare at them. It wasn't unusual for a grateful client to bring in a gift, but Arabella didn't work on cases alone, so they would all know that Rebecca was not a client.

"I wanted to. It's not much, but I wanted to say thank you." She looked around. "Is there somewhere you want me to put them?"

"Oh, yes, let's go into my office," Arabella said. She grabbed her crutch and started to wedge the papers under her arm. Rebecca took the papers from her.

"Don't want them to get creased," she explained.

Arabella found herself speechless. She briefly wondered why she so readily accepted help from Rebecca but shunned it from everyone else. She pushed the thought to one side and turned to lead them towards her office.

"Helen, could you get a vase?" she asked as she crossed the threshold.

Helen looked up from the filing cabinet, from Arabella to Rebecca with a smile.

"Of course, Miss Henley. Would you like tea and coffee?" Helen asked.

"Yes, please," Arabella quickly replied. She purposefully didn't ask Rebecca. If she made the assumption, then the girl would be forced to stay out of politeness.

At the very back of her mind she remembered the numerous tasks she had to do today. Now they seemed to fade in significance. She could take a few minutes.

She gestured to a chair in front of her desk and placed her crutch in their usual place by the filing cabinet. She took the flowers out of Rebecca's hands and looked at them in more detail.

"These are lovely." She'd seen a lot of bouquets in her time in property management, these somehow seemed brighter and fresher than the others that had come before.

"I'm glad you like them, you're hard to buy for," Rebecca said. She took the proffered seat and looked around the office.

"I am not," Arabella argued.

Rebecca chuckled. "Are we disagreeing already? I've barely sat down."

"I'll disagree with you if you make ridiculous statements." Arabella sniffed and put the flowers down gently on the edge of her large desk. She sat in her chair and looked at Rebecca.

"How are you?"

Rebecca paused her inspection of the office and looked at Arabella.

"I'm okay. Getting back out into the real world."

Arabella's heart sunk at the thought of Rebecca only now picking up the pieces and rebuilding her life. The last two weeks of her life had passed in a blur of activity. The thought of Rebecca having slogged through each day ate at her.

She had wanted to get in touch with Rebecca but knew that she had already intruded far too much. She had to keep reminding herself that they were not friends. Circumstance and nothing more had brought them together. Rebecca didn't want to hear about Arabella's life, and she didn't need support from her either. She presumably had hundreds of friends who could offer her much better support.

"Nice office," Rebecca commented. She angled herself around to take in the large, modern space.

"Thank you. I like it."

Rebecca chewed her lip.

"Out with it," Arabella demanded.

The girl laughed. "I was just wondering how to ask something without sounding really nosey."

"That ship has clearly sailed, what do you want to know?"

"Alastair?" Rebecca asked, a light blush appearing on her cheeks.

"Gone," Arabella said.

"Oh." Rebecca sounded surprised. She pointed to Arabella's finger. "I thought you might have had second thoughts?"

Arabella looked at the large diamond ring that still sat on her engagement finger. She toyed with it, spinning it distractedly.

"Not everyone knows, so we're keeping up appearances for a while. He's moved out, but it takes a while to tell everyone, without spooking investors."

"I'll pretend I understand what any of that means." Rebecca grinned. "I'm just glad you're not marrying him. He was an idiot."

Arabella chuckled. "Tell me what you really think, why don't you?"

There was a knock on the door.

"Come in," Arabella called out.

Helen entered the room with a tray. She placed it on the desk and looked at the flowers.

"Would you like me to deal with the flowers for you?" Helen asked.

"Yes, please," Arabella said.

She looked at the tray in front of them. It was the standard client tray with teas, coffee, and biscuits. She picked up the two cups and saucers and placed them on her desk.

"Oh, these are lovely," Helen said as she picked up the flowers.

"Yes, they are. Miss Edwards has good taste," Arabella said, winking at Rebecca.

Helen took the flowers and left the room, closing the door behind her.

"The last time I was called Miss Edwards I was at school. It normally came just before the phrase 'you'll be staying after school'," Rebecca said.

"Were you a bad girl?" Arabella asked, a light heat on her cheeks at the unintended double entendre. "Tea or coffee?" she asked quickly to gloss over the misstep.

"I had my moments," Rebecca said. "Coffee, please. I bet you were a proper goody two-shoes at school."

Arabella poured coffee into one of the cups and pushed it towards Rebecca.

"Help yourself to milk and sugar. Actually, you're right, I was a goody two-shoes as you call it. I was a prefect, then head girl."

Rebecca leaned forward and picked up the tiny silver tongs and started to load up her coffee with sugar cubes.

"Did you ever have detention?"

Arabella poured herself some hot water and added a teabag. She leaned back in her chair while she waited for it to infuse.

"Once," she confessed. "I was caught kissing a boy behind the gym building when I should have been in a science lesson."

"Tell me you weren't missing biology? That would be hilarious." Rebecca stirred her coffee.

"No, sadly it was chemistry. And I didn't find any of that behind the gym building either." She leaned forward and pulled the teabag out of the hot water. "I suppose you were always in detention?"

"Not *always*," Rebecca replied. "But quite a lot."

They shared a quiet laugh. It soon petered out, and the silence became stifling.

"I'm sorry I didn't call," Arabella finally confessed.

"I didn't call either," Rebecca said before she could make further excuses. "I'm sorry for dropping by unannounced. I just wanted to say thank you, again. Not that a single bunch of flowers is any comparison to all that you did for me."

"You don't need to thank me at all. I'm glad I helped in some small way."

Arabella felt a pain in her chest. She knew that this was it, the beginning of a goodbye. They'd said goodbye in the early hours of the twenty-sixth of December, but it hadn't felt permanent. Rebecca was still grieving, and Arabella hadn't wanted to push the issue. But there really was nothing else left to say.

Rebecca chewed her lip.

Arabella cocked her head to the side. She wondered how the girl managed to get by in life with her heart always on her sleeve. "What is it?" she asked.

"Dammit," Rebecca said, "you have to stop doing that."

"I'm not doing anything, you have a tell, you chew on your lip." Arabella gestured to her face.

Rebecca licked her lips and appeared to force her face into a neutral expression. Arabella suddenly wished she hadn't mentioned the tell, it was cute, and she'd miss seeing it. She secretly hoped that Rebecca wouldn't be able to prevent herself from doing it in the future. Should she ever see her again in that future.

"I… was wondering if you could help me? There's this house

thing. A legal thing. I've been looking online, but I really don't understand all the legal jargon. Like, I looked at a lot of websites and none of them made sense. Is that a thing? Are we being conned, so we have to use solicitors? Are all websites really hard to understand so we seek out professional advice? And my mum's solicitor is always busy. He never calls me back. And he's a jerk."

Arabella laughed at the long-winded explanation. "What do you need?"

Rebecca reached into her jacket pocket, produced a couple of envelopes, and slid them across the desk towards Arabella.

"I'm the executor of mum's will. I'm the only one left so it had to be me. And she gave me everything, including the house. But I don't want to keep it. I'm living there now, but I'd like to sell it, but I need… something. Sounds like prostate?"

"A grant of probate," Arabella said.

She took the envelopes, slid her glasses on, and started to read through the familiar documents.

"I'm sorry to call on you again," Rebecca said as she read, "and this is totally not the reason I gave you the flowers. I got the flowers as a thank-you for what you did before. So, don't feel obligated to help me again if you can't, or… don't want to. I can just call the solicitor again—"

"I'm happy to help. Besides, I hear he's a jerk." Arabella nodded towards the plate of biscuits. "Help yourself; let me just read through these documents."

Arabella read the papers, enjoying the companionable silence. Rebecca had only been in the office under five minutes and already she felt like a weight had been lifted. Suddenly the hectic workdays and the sideways glances from staff faded. The end of the engagement hadn't been officially announced, but office gossip pool already had its suspicions. It had been a hectic but fraught couple of weeks.

"I'm sorry, I feel really bad bringing work to you, you're clearly busy," Rebecca apologised again.

"Not too busy to help a friend," Arabella said without thinking.

"Are we friends?" Rebecca asked softly.

Arabella stopped reading and looked up at her. "I thought so?"

Rebecca smiled. Somehow, it lit up the room.

"Cool, I thought you were just being nice because you felt bad for me or something. You look really nice in glasses, by the way."

Arabella stumbled a little upon hearing the compliment. "Th-thank you. And in response to your statement, no, I'm not being nice because I feel bad for you. I'm being nice because I consider us friends. Odd, highly mismatched friends, but friends nonetheless."

Rebecca reached for another biscuit and continued to look around the room. "Do you like these pieces of art?"

Arabella looked at the modern paintings on the wall.

"Not particularly, they came with the office space. Part of the design."

"How long has this been your office?"

Arabella lowered the papers to her desk as she thought about the question.

"I'm not sure. Six, maybe seven years?"

Rebecca looked at her in horror.

"You've been in this office for that long, and you still have the original art on the walls? Art that you don't like? Do you have any personal effects in here?"

Arabella looked around the room, keen to point out a personal item that she could claim. But the truth was, there were none. She worked long hours, but she'd never felt the need to personalise her office space. It was a place to work, somewhere to see clients. Nothing more.

She looked at the paintings on the wall. She'd never really liked them. But then she'd never disliked them enough to take them down.

"You need a grant of probate," Arabella said, trying to change the subject back to a more neutral topic. One where she felt more qualified to answer. "You'll need to fill out a couple of forms, a probate application and an inheritance tax form. You'll need the death certificate and copies of the will. You'll also need to swear an oath."

"Swear an oath?" Rebecca looked at her incredulously.

"The English law system, I'm afraid. After your application has been sent off, you should receive a grant of probate within about ten working days."

"I have to *swear* an *oath*?" Rebecca repeated.

Arabella chuckled. "Yes, just to say that what you are including in your application is true, you're not signing up a cult."

"So, I need to speak to the jerk," Rebecca surmised.

"Unfortunately, yes, you do," Arabella confirmed. "And you'll need to have the house valued in order to fill in the inheritance tax form."

Rebecca slumped back in her chair. "Why is it all so complicated? Like, isn't this the one time when everything should be really easy?"

"Who's your solicitor?" Arabella asked.

"Mr Grindey, at Aldershot, Parker, and Jerk," Rebecca sighed.

"Oh, yes, I know them." Arabella nodded.

Rebecca looked up at her. "Oh, I didn't think about that. I suppose you deal with solicitors a lot?"

"Unfortunately, every single day," Arabella replied. "Robert Grindey is a particular nuisance, very hard to get hold of him. But his secretary is rather amenable. I could contact her and get your case moved to Jonathan Parker? He is much easier to deal with."

"That would be amazing. I've been calling Grindey every day, three or four times a day, and he never calls back."

"Sounds like Robert. I'll give them a call. I can also value your house for you, if you like? That is, if you don't feel it would be a conflict of interest?"

"I'm going to need to get you more flowers," Rebecca said.

"I also accept chocolates," she joked.

"I'll remember that. Seriously, though, that would be amazing. Are you sure you don't mind?"

"Not at all." Arabella reached into her handbag and pulled out her day planner. She opened the book to the correct week and scanned through her appointments. For some reason, she skipped some of her shorter morning slots that were still available and looked at the evening slots. "I'm free next Wednesday at five? Maybe we could have dinner afterwards? It will take me a while to get back to Putney from your neck of the woods."

"Absolutely!" Rebecca enthused. "I'll make you dinner. Any allergies? Other than sugar, salt, and grease? You know, anything that makes food actually taste good."

Arabella laughed at the comment on her healthy eating.

"I like to eat well, I'm not young like you. if I ate all the junk you ate on the drive back, I'd swell up like a balloon."

Rebecca opened her mouth to reply and quickly slammed it shut again. Arabella wondered if it had been a compliment or a joke that had been on her mind.

"Well, then I'll make something healthy. Anything I should avoid? I don't want to kill you off before I get that grant of probate."

Arabella shook her head. "Thank you, your concern for my wellbeing, as always, is heart-warming. But, no, I don't have any allergies."

"Great, I better let you get on with some work. Sorry to barge in and add to your work pile." Rebecca stood up. She reached forward and snagged another biscuit from the plate.

Arabella stood up as well. "It was good to see you."

"Do you need the address, or do you still have it from when you stalked me the last time?" Rebecca joked.

"I still have it, is that why you're moving?" she replied with a grin.

"Nah, it's more that the house is on a giant sinkhole. Don't tell my estate agent." Rebecca winked. She reached forward and picked up the documents that Arabella had been reading. And then snagged a third biscuit. "I'll see myself out."

"Good, the biscuit budget can't handle much more."

Rebecca waved her hand dismissively and left the office, laughing as she went.

Arabella flopped back into her chair. Her cheeks were aching from all the smiling and laughing, despite the short visit. She wondered how Rebecca could disarm her so easily. It wasn't in Arabella's nature to relax around new people. There was something different about Rebecca, something warm and down-to-earth.

She looked at the new entry in her day planner. Butterflies started to flutter in her stomach. Dinner with Rebecca wasn't a new thing, they'd eaten together before. But somehow this felt different.

She blew out a breath and slammed the day planner closed.

Come on, Arabella. Get yourself together.

CHAPTER 27

REBECCA WALKED around the house one last time. She'd let things go a bit in the last couple of weeks, so she'd spent the entire day clearing used mugs and discarded bras from almost every room.

The house had felt pretty big and lonely, and so she'd gone through a phase of making every room feel homely. Reading, drawing, surfing the internet on her favourite chair in each room. Before she knew it, she'd trashed every room.

And now Arabella was coming, so Rebecca had spent nine hours solidly tidying up and cleaning. She had even scrubbed the grout in the guest bathroom. Because Arabella seemed to demand perfection without even opening her mouth.

She was petrified that she would overlook something, but it was no use worrying now. It was two minutes to five, and Rebecca was trying her best to look like she had been casually waiting and not running around like a lunatic all day.

She'd got a pretty cup and saucer from the cupboard and drunk half a cup of coffee from it. She then placed the cup and saucer next to an open, old-fashioned hardback of *Great Expectations* on the coffee table in the living room. A tartan blanket was folded neatly beside the place she had supposedly been sitting on the sofa. She couldn't help but take a few pictures of her setup; stock images of lifestyle aesthetics like this sold pretty well.

She caught a look at herself in the mirror. She'd had a shower an hour before, scrubbing away the smell of detergents and replacing them with the posh scents she usually only used on dates. They probably still weren't quite up to Arabella's standards, but at least it wasn't some cheap celebrity perfume that smelt like an explosion in a flower garden for half an hour before wearing off.

She'd put her hair up in a messy bun, spending far longer than she should have pulling individual strands of hair down to frame her face in a theoretically casual way. She wore a long-sleeved, oversized sweater. It was cream and had a few designer rips in it. She adjusted the neck a few times, making sure that her exposed shoulder looked casual enough.

She'd put on her smart, skinny blue jeans, too. She didn't want to look like she made no effort, after all. Casual could quickly tip into not giving a damn, and Rebecca wanted to look good, not like she'd made much of an effort, but still good.

The truth was, she'd made an enormous effort and she was now utterly exhausted and tense as she waited for Arabella's arrival.

She looked at the book and coffee set-up and rolled her eyes. It was too much. She rushed over to the table but paused as she stretched out her arms. Was it too much? And why did it matter so much to her?

In her heart she knew exactly why it mattered. But she

couldn't admit to it. Down that path led a lot of trouble and heartbreak.

The doorbell sounded. She jumped in surprise. She looked at the wall clock, it was exactly five. Of course, Arabella would be perfectly on time.

Rebecca glanced at her reflection once more before reminding herself that there was nothing else that could be done about her appearance now. She hurried down the hallway on tiptoes, not wanting to leave Arabella waiting, but also not wanting to appear to be in a rush.

She opened the door and stood to one side.

"Hi, come in," she said.

As Arabella entered the house, Rebecca took a moment to appreciate the light grey skirt suit she was wearing. She caught a whiff of expensive-smelling perfume. It took her a few moments longer than it should have to notice that something was missing.

"Hey, you don't have your crutch. Or your cast!"

"Nothing gets by you," Arabella kidded. She looked happy, a real smile gracing her lips and an extra bounce in her step.

"The cast was removed a couple of days ago. It still hurts but I'm healing and need to put weight on it and strengthen the muscles."

Rebecca found herself staring at Arabella's legs. She was allowed to do that, right? She was just noticing that the cast was gone. For a while. Really noticing.

"I'll be happy to get back into heels," Arabella said, shaking Rebecca from her inappropriate gaze.

"Not too soon, though. You don't want to put your recovery back," Rebecca pointed out.

"You sound like my father." Arabella rolled her eyes and

placed her bag on the empty hallway table. She took out a leather file and a camera. "If you like, I could take pictures now as well as the valuation? That way, if you choose us to represent you, we wouldn't have to bother you again with taking photos for the advertisement."

Rebecca liked the idea of Arabella bothering her again, but she suspected Arabella didn't want to make more journeys than was necessary.

"Sounds good."

"Excellent." Arabella looked at her expectantly. "Do you want to show me around?"

Rebecca nodded and hurried to the doorway to the living room. She stepped inside, and Arabella followed.

"Um, this is... obviously... the living room."

"Is that fire gas or electric?"

Rebecca cocked her hear to one side as she regarded the device. She had no idea. Her mum had hardly used it. To her, it was just an object in the room, something she didn't even see anymore.

Arabella stepped closer to the fireplace and glanced at it.

"Gas," she answered her own question and made a note with her fountain pen on her leather-covered notepad. She took out a laser measuring device and placed it on the wall to get the dimensions of the room.

Arabella glanced at the coffee and book set-up that Rebecca had spent time crafting and smirked. Rebecca wondered what it meant. Had Arabella seen through her?

Of course she knew it had been set up. Estate agents must frequently see people pretending to live the perfect life in the perfect home, fresh coffee brewing and bread baking in the oven.

She felt a little stupid for trying to pull the wool over Arabella's eyes like that. Even if she did genuinely drink coffee from that cup and saucer and had read that book. Once. Eight years ago.

They moved into the dining room, and Arabella continued to take notes as Rebecca silently waited.

She counted how many rooms there were and dreaded the idea of pointlessly listing them all. Kitchen. Bedroom. Bedroom. Yet another bedroom. Bathroom. Hallway. Was the hallway even a room? Would Arabella think she was silly for calling it a room?

She wondered when she had gotten so nervous around Arabella.

Arabella looked out of the double doors and into the garden. "Is there a side gate?"

"Yes, and a garage," Rebecca replied. *Good, you sound like you know what you're talking about now, keep it up.*

"And which side of the garden is yours?"

Rebecca frowned. "Um, what?"

Arabella pointed towards the nearest fence with her pen. "One of these fences is your responsibility to maintain, the other side is your neighbours."

Rebecca couldn't remember anything ever being mentioned about the fences. Nor could she remember them ever being replaced or repaired. Was this a thing? Ownership of fences? Was she such a bad adult that she didn't know? Was she the only person who didn't know? Were the neighbours laughing at her lack of fence maintenance knowledge?

"It will be in the legal documentation, I can find out there," Arabella said. "Oh, is it freehold or leasehold?"

"Freehold," Rebecca said, happy she had something to contribute.

Arabella scribbled some more notes down before looking up at Rebecca. "Next? The kitchen?" she questioned, pointing towards the next door.

Rebecca nodded and led them into the kitchen. This time she didn't announce the room, she assumed the sink would give it away. She leant awkwardly against the kitchen worktop, watching as Arabella walked around and made notes.

"You're very quiet," Arabella commented. "Not like you."

Rebecca smiled, relieved at the change of topic. "I don't want to interrupt your work."

"I'm just making notes, feel free to talk to me," Arabella said, still scribbling down more observations.

Rebecca's mind raced at a hundred miles per hour to come up with something to say. When had she lost the ability to make conversation?

"I thought I'd make omelettes for dinner," she eventually said. "Healthy but awesome, because I make the best omelettes in the world."

"That sounds lovely, I love omelettes," Arabella replied. "Shall we go upstairs?"

Rebecca blinked for a moment. Her mouth felt unnaturally dry. A split second later she realised what Arabella meant, but she also realised that she'd been still and silent a moment too long.

"Um, maybe I should start dinner?" Rebecca offered. "I'm sure you can find your way around up there, there's no secret passageway to the east tower. What you see is what you get."

Arabella regarded her for a moment, a small smile curling her lips.

"Okay, I'll call if I need anything," she said. She walked out into the hallway and made her way up the creaky staircase.

Rebecca let out a long sigh. She needed to get herself together. Spending the whole day worrying and preparing for Arabella's visit hadn't prepared her at all, it had just panicked her.

She'd somehow lost the ability to speak, which was a problem when you'd invited someone over for dinner. It wasn't done to sit in silence and then kick the guest out the moment they swallowed the last bite. Besides, she wanted Arabella to be there. She wanted to have a nice meal and discuss things.

She just needed to get herself under control.

It's okay, it's just Arabella, you can do this, she reminded herself.

CHAPTER 28

ARABELLA WALKED into the master bedroom and had a quick look around. Everything seemed quite normal. London was awash with 1930s semi-detached houses, and as she'd observed on Christmas Eve, this one seemed no different. A little rundown, but nothing that some maintenance couldn't take care of.

She turned and walked into the second bedroom, pausing in the doorway. It was clearly Rebecca's room. Somehow it felt wrong being in there without Rebecca's presence, even though she knew she had permission.

She was also insanely curious.

Photograph collages filled the walls. Arabella looked at them with interest. Some were from the local area, some were of inanimate objects, some she couldn't even identify what they were, just shapes and colours. She stepped further into the room, taking more of an interest in the personal effects than she normally would on an appraisal tour.

A desk in front of the window was covered with random

objects, from comics to perfume bottles. She smiled, Rebecca certainly had a lot of interests. It was fascinating to get a peek into her mind and her hobbies.

She caught herself snooping, so she lifted up her notepad and started to make some notes about the room. She used the laser measure and drew a small diagram, adding in the radiator and the window. House hunters loved accurate floor plans.

Arabella wondered how long Rebecca had lived in the house. Had she grown up in it? Had she moved out and come back when her mother took ill? Were these questions that Arabella had any business asking? It wasn't relevant to the house sale, and yet she wanted to know.

She turned around and walked out of the room before the urge to snoop became any stronger. It felt wrong, especially knowing that Rebecca was just downstairs, cooking her a meal. She wondered, not for the first time, why she had suggested dinner. A war was taking place inside of her. Part of her was desperate to stay away from Rebecca, part of her was coming up with new reasons to see her.

"Everything okay?"

Arabella turned around on the landing to see Rebecca walking up the stairs. She was wiping her hands with a tea towel.

"Absolutely, just finished," she said, relieved she hadn't been found in Rebecca's room.

"Great, I was just going to ask what you'd like to drink?" Rebecca started listing the entire drinks aisle of the local supermarket.

"Orange juice sounds lovely," Arabella picked one to prevent the never-ending list from sucking all of the oxygen from the small hallway.

They walked down the stairs and into the kitchen.

Rebecca poured two glasses of orange juice while Arabella activated her iPad and had a look at some of the local property prices. She'd done some research before leaving the office, probably a bit more than was technically required for an inheritance tax form. But she wanted to ensure that Rebecca was going to get the best price possible, she didn't want the girl to go with some local charlatan and settle for a quick sale.

"So, how many pennies is it worth? I know it's not in great shape."

Arabella was pleased that Rebecca had mentioned the matter of upkeep. It was always a sensitive subject to mention. Telling a house owner that their beloved home was looking a bit tired wasn't easy.

"I was going to mention that," Arabella said. "I'm going to give you two valuations. One is if you sell as is, the other is if you attend to some cosmetic issues."

Rebecca nodded and gestured towards the hob. "I am listening, I'm just going to get on with dinner while you talk."

"No problem," Arabella said. She made some notes in her book as she came to the final valuations.

"You're probably looking at 380,000 pounds if you sell as it is, but, with some work, I think you could easily get as much as 430,000."

Rebecca dropped the spatula she'd been holding. "What?!"

Arabella opened her mouth to repeat the figures, but Rebecca retrieved the spatula and started waving it towards her.

"No, never mind, I heard. Are you seriously telling me that I could get fifty *grand* more if I... what exactly?"

"New carpets, decorate all the rooms. I'd recommend a new bathroom suite, and then fix a few things like the windowsills, tidy up the garden, maybe repair the broken paving slab on the front path."

"That sounds expensive," Rebecca said as she tossed the spatula into the sink and picked a new one out of a drawer.

"Not fifty thousand pounds expensive," Arabella pointed out.

Rebecca started to pour the whisked eggs into a frying pan, her mouth contorted as she considered the matter.

"Put it this way. You can get a very nice bathroom suite for under a thousand pounds. Carpets throughout, depends on what you choose, but around two thousand for something nice. If you want to save some money, then you can do the decorating yourself. You're artsy, I'm sure you can paint walls easily enough."

"You make it sound so easy. Lick of paint, new bath, bish bash bosh. Fifty grand."

"I used to flip houses," Arabella explained. "Before I became so involved in the family business. I'd buy run-down properties and fix them up. You can make quite good money out of it."

Rebecca laughed. "I can't see you tiling a bathroom yourself. Did you have a team of decorators to do all the hard work?"

Arabella closed her notepad and stared at Rebecca with mock anger.

"I'll have you know, young lady, that I'm very handy."

"Uh-oh, I'm a young lady now." Rebecca chuckled.

"Well, you're certainly younger than me," Arabella pointed out. "But anyway, let's not drift from the subject, you were slighting my DIY skills."

"Well, I've yet to see any evidence of your supposed handiness. This could all be bluster." Rebecca managed to play along while still cooking the dinner. Which smelt fantastic and had

Arabella wondering the last time someone cooked a meal for her outside of a restaurant.

"I'm an expert wallpaper hanger," Arabella said with a flourish. "Many have commented on my neat edges."

"Ha!" Rebecca scoffed with a wink. "Wallpaper is easy, what about the hard work? What about painting a ceiling? Laying a floor?"

"I've laid a wooden floor, I even own my own jigsaw."

Rebecca turned the hob off and picked up the two plates of steaming omelette and crisp-looking salad. She gestured her head towards the dining room. Arabella grabbed the two glasses of juice and walked into the dining room, surprised to see the table had been expertly laid in the short amount of time she'd been upstairs.

"You laid a wooden floor, eh?" Rebecca placed the plates on the table.

Arabella sat down and placed the linen napkin on her lap, breathing in the delicious smell emanating from her plate.

"I did," she replied. "It's remarkable what you can learn from YouTube."

Rebecca chuckled. "I never thought of you as someone who'd get hands on. I'd thought you'd get a man in to do it all."

"I don't like asking anyone else to do something I couldn't do myself, where possible. And some builders see a woman and add fifty percent to the price. I like convenience, but I like profit margins even more. The first house I renovated cost me huge amounts, and with the mortgage payments and the tax, I walked away with one hundred and three pounds. For thirteen months' work."

She picked up her knife and fork and started to slice into the fluffy omelette. "This looks incredible."

"Just something I learnt to make in Spain," Rebecca dismissed. "But wow, that's a long time for not a lot of money. I can see why you started doing it yourself. I've never really learnt how to do that kind of stuff. Even if a light bulb is out I'm worried I'll electrocute myself. And Mum was useless; I can't even remember the last time we decorated."

Arabella moaned at the delicious flavour of the omelette. "This is amazing. I'd say you should give me the recipe, but I'm to cooking what you are to DIY."

"What about learning from YouTube?"

Arabella shook her head.

"No, there's something about my brain that takes perfectly to understanding how to rewire a house, how to tile a feature wall, or even how to fix a bannister rail. But give me some basic ingredients and step-by-step instructions and it will all go to hell by step three."

"I could teach you how to cook," Rebecca offered. "I taught my mum to cook and she was useless. I had to learn to cook when I was a kid or I would have starved to death. The second I was tall enough to see the counter, I was making meals."

Arabella could see a crossroads ahead. Down one path lurked more time with Rebecca, the opportunity to become closer friends. Down the other path, sensible retreat from a situation that she knew was becoming something she wasn't sure she was ready for.

"That sounds great." Her traitorous heart answered before her head could formulate an excuse. "And I could teach you DIY."

You imbecile, Arabella's brain informed her.

"Really? That would be amazing," Rebecca enthused. "I mean, I'm all for increasing the value of this place, but I have no idea how. I'd really love your guidance. And, hey, you'll be selling it, so you're totally incentivised to help me increase the asking price."

Arabella raised her eyebrow. "Will I be selling it?"

"Well, yeah, I don't know any other estate agents…" Rebecca paused. "Unless… unless you don't want to? Or this isn't right for Henley's? I know you're a posh firm, but you have a branch on the high street near here so I thought—"

"I'd love to," Arabella reassured. "I just hadn't assumed that we'd get the business. I thought you might speak with others before making a decision."

"Oh, you totally have the business," Rebecca reassured. "I trust you. And I need as much money as possible. I know you won't con me."

Arabella reached for the glass of juice, wondering about whether or not it was appropriate to ask why Rebecca needed the money. Her brow furrowed.

"I have to pay off Cutter Carter," Rebecca explained. "The drug drop went bad, and if I don't find the money within the next couple of months…" Rebecca broke off and started laughing hard. "Oh my god, you should have seen your face!"

Arabella realized she was gawping and put her glass down. "That was very mean."

"No, that was hilarious," Rebecca said, wiping tears from her eyes.

Arabella smiled despite the joke at her expense. She had to admit, it was a little funny.

"Fine, why do you need the money? Presumably not because of your ties to the mob?"

"No. No mob ties. I need the money for my adventure!" Rebecca exclaimed.

She dabbed her mouth with her napkin and got up from her chair. She crossed the room, opened a drawer in the sideboard, and took out a large white envelope.

Arabella watched her with interest. Rebecca was beaming as she poured the contents of the envelope onto the table.

"When Mum first got sick, I was just about to go on a backpacking trip around the world. I'd worked like a machine and saved enough money to finance part of it, planning to do odd jobs here and there to pay for the rest as I went. But the week before I was due to fly to my first stop, she was diagnosed with cancer."

Rebecca placed maps, brochures, leaflets, and scribbled notes down on the table.

"Mum made me promise that I'd one day go and travel like I always wanted to. Life's too short and all that."

Arabella pushed her half-eaten plate of food to one side, suddenly not quite so hungry. She picked up a piece of paper and read a long list of country names with wide eyes.

"So, I'm doing it. Me and Mum talked about all the things I should see and all the things I should experience. I wrote a list, like a bucket list. It made her happy to help me plan the trip, and now I'm in a situation where I can go. Nothing is keeping me here."

Arabella felt her hand tremble slightly as she held the piece of paper.

"Absolutely," she agreed.

She couldn't believe that she had just managed to find a friend, someone who she really enjoyed spending time with, someone who had opened her eyes to a new way of living her life. And now that person was leaving.

"Isn't it a bit dangerous?" Arabella asked. She put the paper down and picked up a leaflet for a tourist bus trip in Egypt. "Like Egypt, I'm pretty sure there's a Home Office advisory about Egypt."

"Yeah, but that's mainly Sinai. It's fine." Rebecca plucked the leaflet from Arabella's hand. "Besides, the more money I get from the house sale, the less I'll stay in cheap dorms and hostels."

Arabella felt a panic sweep through her. She wanted to talk Rebecca out of it, but she knew it would come out wrong. This was clearly something she had been planning for years, at the behest of her dying mother. She couldn't just stand by and let her go backpacking across Egypt and get herself sold for a camel. Could she?

If the final sale price of the house was going to directly correlate with Rebecca's safety on her ridiculous mission to see the world, then Arabella would make damn sure that the house sold for as much as possible.

She briefly wondered if it would be possible to delay the sale somehow. Surely Rebecca couldn't go if the house didn't sell at all. She wondered if there was any subsidence in the area that she would be legally bound to mention to any potential purchasers. Maybe there was a sinkhole?

"Are you okay?" Rebecca asked. "You've gone pale. Is something wrong with dinner?"

Arabella blinked and cleared her mind.

"I'm fine, just a little tired. It's been a long day." She pulled her plate closer. "And dinner is delicious."

Rebecca smiled. She swept all of the paperwork up with her hands and started stuffing it back into the envelope.

"So, do we have a deal?"

"What deal?" Arabella asked, a forkful of food paused in front of her mouth.

Rebecca rolled her eyes.

"The deal we just discussed. I teach you to cook, you teach me DIY."

"Oh!" Arabella remembered the moments before the terrifying discovery that Rebecca planned to get herself murdered in some godforsaken country.

"Yes, of course." She ate the food, chewing slowly as she began to formulate a plan.

She swallowed. "Actually, maybe I should come over and help you with the DIY projects? It's been a while since I've gotten my teeth into a project like this, and hands-on teaching is always more effective."

"Really? Are you sure?"

"Absolutely. What are friends for?"

"That would be amazing." Rebecca sipped her juice. "You know, you may have been a monumental pain in the butt on our car trip, but I'm so glad we met."

Arabella plucked a small piece of lettuce from her plate and threw it at Rebecca's face.

CHAPTER 29

REBECCA SAT at the top of the platform ladders and let out a sigh. She dabbed her paintbrush at the wall, wondering how Arabella made it look so easy while she was struggling. She looked down at where Arabella was running her paintbrush neatly along the wall, just above the skirting board.

"Why does my paint look blotchy while yours looks professional?" she complained.

"Practice." Arabella stood and squinted towards the top of the wall. "You have too much paint on your brush."

"You literally *just* told me I had too little."

"And now you have too much." Arabella grinned. "Paint is fickle."

"Paint is something," Rebecca mumbled.

Arabella returned to her kneeling position and continued to paint.

Rebecca stared at the wall, hating how it was embarrassing her in front of Arabella. She was artsy, she was creative, but she couldn't paint a wall to save her life.

"Did you call the builder I suggested about the garden?" Arabella asked.

"I did, he said he will come on Monday," Rebecca replied.

She had to admit, she was enjoying herself. The conspiracy the paint had against her aside, it was homely. Just two friends, decorating a house and chatting.

Although she suspected that she was mainly enjoying the company. Arabella was fast becoming a permanent fixture in her mind.

After the successful dinner, where she had managed to kick off the nerves and have a normal conversation, Rebecca's mind had been preoccupied with thoughts of Arabella. Every day seemed to consist of casually wondering what Arabella would think or say about something.

She knew what it meant. She wasn't stupid. But she also knew that Arabella was straight and simply being a good friend. Something that Rebecca was in short supply of.

She had friends. Loads of friends. But her friends were either young and immature, or completely focused on their careers. Not to mention that Rebecca hadn't been a great friend lately. Her life had been so hectic that she'd not been very good at keeping up with friends. And when her mum had died, she received a flood of condolence text messages, emails, and Facebook updates. And then everyone had stayed away. Worried about how Rebecca was dealing with the loss and not wanting to intrude.

So, life had been a little lonely. She knew she could pick up the phone and call someone, but the truth was that she didn't want to. She wanted to stay in her little cocoon. She wanted to paint the dining room on a Sunday morning with Arabella.

"So," Arabella said with what sounded like fake casualness. "Travel."

"Yep." Rebecca scraped her paint brush against her tin, trying to remove the excess.

"You seem to have it all planned."

"I do. I've been thinking about it for a long time." Rebecca could sense Arabella's wariness.

She suspected that Arabella thought the idea of travelling around the world and staying in cheap hostels was childish and dangerous.

"Have you travelled much?" she asked, trying to change the subject.

"Some." Arabella shuffled along the floor to continue painting the skirting board. "Mainly for work these days."

"Just locations where a gazillionaire needs a holiday home to get away from the paparazzi?" Rebecca joked.

"I don't deal with anyone below a kazillionaire," Arabella replied.

"Of course, you must maintain standards."

"Indeed."

"Is there anywhere you haven't seen that you want to see? Something to tick off the bucket list?"

"I don't have a bucket list," Arabella said.

Rebecca paused, her paintbrush centimetres away from the wall.

"You don't have a bucket list?"

"No. Too much pressure. I could die tomorrow. I don't want to be laying in the street after being hit by a bus and thinking that I never got to see the sunset over the Sahara, or the Northern Lights. I'd be quite disappointed enough that I'd been hit by a bus without the added pressure."

"That… that's *so* pessimistic."

"I've never been known for my optimism," Arabella confessed. "I wasn't exactly encouraged by my parents to dream big. I had a path laid out for me and I'm exactly where I'm supposed to be."

Rebecca balanced her paintbrush on the tin and stepped down the ladder.

"You may be a part of some grand plan for Henley's to take over the London property market, but surely you've thought 'I wanna do that' at some point in your life? Not everything revolves around work. You do get some free time."

Arabella looked up at Rebecca. "You've stopped painting."

"Forget the painting, you've just told me that you have no dreams." Rebecca shook her head in exasperation. How could Arabella focus on painting at a time like this?

"I have dreams, they just don't match up to your expectations of the dreams I should have." Arabella put her paintbrush down. "I dream that we'll hire a really good receptionist next time, so that my clients are offered drinks in a timely manner. I dream that Mrs Taylor will stop messing about and just buy the damn house on Sycamore Avenue. I dream that—"

"These are all work-related. Come on, I know you have a life outside of work." Rebecca paused. "Wait, you do have a life outside of work, don't you? You must have a hobby, right?"

"I… like gardening," Arabella admitted as if it were a struggle to come up with anything.

Rebecca stared at her.

"I do!"

"You liar, you just picked that out of thin air. I can see it in your eyes."

Arabella turned away. She picked up the paintbrush and continued her work.

"We're not talking about me, we're talking about you and your travel plans."

Rebecca looked at Arabella's tense posture. She realised that she had upset her with her suggestion that she had nothing outside of work. She wondered if it were true. Arabella was the kind of person who would live for her work.

"I suggest you read the Foreign Office's online travel guidance," Arabella said. "There's a lot of information on there about countries that are not safe to visit. You can't just gallivant around the planet as if there are no consequences."

Rebecca felt her jaw open. "Gallivant?"

"Yes, it's hardly the most sensible option, is it?" Arabella scoffed. "Coming into a large inheritance, you should be putting it aside for the future. Buying a home, creating security. But you're going to spend it all on seeing the world. And then you'll presumably come back here with nothing to show for it but some knickknacks that you collected on your travels. Possibly a drunken tattoo."

"Wow," Rebecca breathed. "You really have that low an opinion of me?"

Arabella turned around. Her eyes widened as if she only just realised what she had said.

"I'm sorry, I'm sorry, I didn't mean that. That was... harsh. I apologise."

Rebecca furrowed her brow. Arabella's apology seemed sincere enough, but she was hurt. She knew the insinuation hadn't come from nowhere. There was an element of Arabella's true feelings in there.

"So, you think I should buy a small house and get a job, right?"

"It doesn't matter what I think," Arabella said softly.

"No, it does. I know I'm young, you think of me as a child compared to you and all your adult accomplishments. You think I should settle down and get on the career path, don't you? I suppose not having a stable career makes me a bit of a failure in your eyes, right?"

"I never said that." Arabella put her paintbrush down and climbed to her feet. "And I don't feel like that."

"It's okay, I get it. I know we're different people," Rebecca continued. "You have your life together, I don't. I'm a dreamer, you're practical. I'm just some loser with fanciful ideas about travelling that will amount to nothing important."

"Don't change a thing about you," Arabella said forcefully. "I shouldn't have said what I said, I'm sorry. It comes from a place of fear, I worry about you. But I don't have any right to tell you what to do."

"You worry about me?" Her breath caught in her throat.

"Of course I do. You're about to sell everything and pack a bag and go god knows where to see god knows what. You won't know where you're going to be sleeping from week to week. Knowing you, you'll walk into some war zone and get yourself killed!"

Rebecca saw real fear in Arabella's eyes. She noted that her hands were balled into tight fists.

"Yeah, but it's a *really* great bag," she joked to defuse the tension.

Arabella shook her head and marched out of the room. Rebecca rolled her eyes at herself. She always reverted to joking when she really ought to be serious. And now Arabella was mad at her.

She walked out of the room and into the kitchen where Arabella had her back to her.

"Hey, I'm sorry, I shouldn't have joked like that."

Rebecca waiting for a reply, but none came.

"I just joke when things are tense, you know?"

She shifted her weight from foot to foot.

"And it is a great bag…"

She heard a sniffle. Arabella's shoulders shook slightly.

Rebecca stared in shock.

"Are you… are you crying?" She quickly walked around to get a look at Arabella's face.

As soon as she moved, Arabella moved as well.

"Stop turning," Rebecca ordered.

Arabella ignored her. They spun around a few times like children playing chase.

Eventually, she took a hold of Arabella's shoulders and forced her to make eye contact. Red eyes and wet cheeks looked back at her. She wondered what on earth she had said to upset her so much.

"I don't want you to get hurt," Arabella mumbled. She turned to shield her face. "I keep thinking that you're going to go wander into a minefield or get taken hostage by ISIS, or… or die of exposure on a sand dune!"

Rebecca pulled her into a hug. Arabella struggled slightly. Rebecca knew she felt embarrassed at becoming upset but held on tighter. She waited for Arabella to stop resisting and give in to it.

"I don't know where you think I'm going," Rebecca whispered into her hair. "I want to see the Coliseum, bathe in the waters off Bali, and see the Sydney Opera House. I don't have any intention of wondering around Syria. I'm not going to do a weekend tour of Mosul."

"They have terrorist attacks in Bali," Arabella whispered.

"They have terrorist attacks in London," Rebecca countered. "You're in more danger here than I am."

"Thanks, now I'm worried about that, too," Arabella mumbled. She adjusted her stance and wrapped her arms around Rebecca, holding her tight.

Rebecca swallowed nervously. She wondered what to do. Arabella didn't seem like the kind of person to just break down in tears. This had obviously been bothering her for a while. Rebecca wondered if Arabella maybe felt something for her. Her heart soared at the very thought.

"Come with me," Rebecca suggested.

Arabella took a step backwards. Rebecca felt the loss keenly.

"Come with you?" Her brow knitted.

"Travel with me," Rebecca said.

Arabella wiped at her tears as she chuckled. "I can't do that. I have… I… I just can't do that."

Rebecca started to feel stupid for even suggesting it.

"I know, I— I just offered so you can see for yourself that it's safe."

Arabella took another step backwards.

"I'm sorry, I shouldn't have become so emotional. I'm not sure what's wrong with me."

Rebecca could see that she was planning to make her escape. She had seconds to decide on whether she wanted to let her go or bring up the elephant in the room.

"I think you do know," Rebecca said.

Arabella looked hesitant before shaking her head.

"Just tired, I'm sure. It's been a busy week."

Rebecca wasn't about to accept that excuse. "I think it's more than that."

She couldn't control the shaking in her voice. Nor could she predict what Arabella's reaction would be, and it frightened her. Would she laugh it off? Would she run a mile? Gay paranoia was a thing, Rebecca had seen it before.

Arabella looked at her in surprise, her mouth opening and closing as she struggled to find something to say.

Suddenly, she grabbed her handbag from the kitchen worktop and hurried away. Rebecca momentarily considered running after her, but she knew that emotions were high, which made it a bad idea. She watched as Arabella rushed through the front door and out of her life.

CHAPTER 30

ARABELLA TOOK off her reading glasses and tossed them onto the desk. Reading the fine print on legal contracts was the bane of her existence. And, to her mind, the sole reason why she now had to wear glasses.

Usually she'd pass the tedious task on to one of the juniors, but she was keeping herself busy. Anything to avoid the voice in the back of her head whispering and ridiculing her for running away from Rebecca the previous month. And ignoring her calls. And passing the paperwork for Rebecca's sale on to someone else.

Helen burst into the office. Arabella jumped.

"Sorry, couldn't knock," Helen explained.

She held a large package wrapped in brown paper. It was nearly as tall as she was and only a couple of inches thick.

Arabella got up and walked over to help her.

"It was just delivered; are you expecting something?"

"I ordered a new phone case, but I'm assuming that's not it," Arabella said as they leaned the heavy package against the wall.

"Not unless screen sizes have really gotten out of control. Can I get you anything else?"

Arabella shook her head, distracted by the package. She heard the click of the door closing as Helen left the room. She started looking around the package for a delivery note. She tore at the clear plastic address label and pulled out the paper. Her heart stopped when she saw the sender's name.

Rebecca Edwards.

She took a deep breath and put the delivery slip on her desk. She regarded the package suspiciously for a moment. Then, she plucked the scissors out of her pen pot and carefully sliced the top and sides of the cardboard.

It flopped open, revealing several large picture frames. She frowned and separated the first two. Her eyebrows raised in shock and she gasped. The frames contained large photographs of the beautiful vista they'd seen when travelling in Spain.

She pulled the first frame out of the cardboard packaging and held it in front of her. It was just as beautiful as she remembered it, the sun hitting the distant mountains and casting light across the land. She placed the first frame in front of her desk and quickly picked up the second. It was another shot of the view, but from another angle. The sun had lowered a little more giving a dramatically different effect.

She held the frame up with both hands and turned to look at the dreary artwork on her walls. She walked to the other side of the room, placing the frame below the painting she disliked the most.

She returned to the cardboard box and pulled apart another two frames. An envelope fluttered to the floor.

Scooping the envelope up, she walked over to her desk and slumped into her chair. She was scared. Part of her desperately didn't want to open the envelope, afraid of what Rebecca's words would say.

But then she knew the curiosity would be too much for her to leave it unopened. She held her breath for a moment before plunging in. She pulled out a piece of paper and a photo.

The photograph was of her. She was smiling and standing in front of the vista, having just discovered that Rebecca was a professional photographer. She'd been enjoying watching the girl in her element. And being told that she was beautiful. She placed the photo and the envelope down on the desk and held the paper in shaking hands.

She unfolded the letter and took a deep breath before reading.

Arabella,

I had intended to give you these after we'd painted the dining room. You desperately needed new artwork for your office. If you don't like them, then feel free to give them away, or even throw them away. I include my favourite photo but assumed that you aren't narcissistic enough to want it blown up to a metre high like the others.

I miss you.

Rebecca

Relief swept over her. She'd expected ranting and raving, a claim that she was running away from her feelings. A hastily scribbled note about being homophobic. But Rebecca was as kind as ever, not even mentioning her terrible behaviour, running away in the middle of a project and ignoring the girl's subsequent calls.

The door burst open for a second time, and she opened her mouth to berate Helen for scaring her again. But it wasn't Helen entering the room, it was Alastair.

"I need you to sign these," he said without preamble, tossing some legal documents onto her desk.

She discreetly folded Rebecca's note and slid it into her desk drawer. She picked up the documents and started to look at them.

"The solicitor won't talk to me about anything to do with the sale of the cottage unless you sign that. Pedantic old man," Alastair grumbled.

He sat on the edge of the desk, picked up a stray elastic band, and started to play with it.

Arabella nodded in understanding.

"I'm sorry, I'd forgotten to tell him that you would be dealing with the cottage. My fault." She picked up her fountain pen and started to read through the document thoroughly, never one to sign anything without reading it.

"Not a problem," Alastair replied. "How have you been?"

"Well. Busy."

"As you like it."

She looked at him.

"Alastair," she warned.

He held up his hands. "Just a comment, I don't mean anything by it."

Strangely enough, her relationship with Alastair had actually improved since the break-up. They fought less, listened to each other more. The pressure of the wedding and the new life they were embarking on had vanished, and, instead, they were just two people working together to separate their lives.

It reminded her that Alastair did actually care for her in his own strange way. Despite initially not wanting to break off the engagement, he was now happy to do his bit to split their interests.

She returned her attention to the document and picked up where she had left off.

The elastic band pinged from Alastair's fingers and landed on the floor. Arabella rolled her eyes as he bent down and picked it up.

She signed the document and looked up to hand it back to him.

She paused in fright. He was holding the photograph of her in his hand, looking at it curiously.

"If you want my advice," Alastair said, as though he could read her thoughts, "you'll find whoever it is who can make you look this happy and build a life with them."

He took the proffered documents with one hand and held out the photograph with the other.

"I'll take that under advisement," she said. She snatched the photo from his hand and dropped it into her desk drawer.

"Do," Alastair said firmly. "You deserve to be happy. I know I never made you that happy. I wish I did, but I know I didn't. I have a suspicion who can, and I think you should grab them with both hands. Life is short."

He turned around before she could formulate a reply.

"Thanks for these." He waved the documents in the air. "I'll try to get more than a button and an old shoe for the cottage, but I can't promise anything."

CHAPTER 31

"Are you going to bite me?" Rebecca asked the little crawling insect that was working its way up the handle of the shovel. "Because I'm really not into gardening and that's really going to put a massive downer on the whole thing if you end up being a bitey insect."

She leant in close and looked at it. "You totally have teeth, put those away, friend."

"Maybe it doesn't speak English?"

Rebecca jumped in fear and dropped the bug-infested shovel. She spun around to face the unexpected sound of Arabella's voice.

"The gate was left open and I heard you talking," her visitor explained, gesturing to the open side entrance to the back garden.

Rebecca's heart slammed against her rib cage. She knew sending the photos had been a bad idea. She'd gotten them printed a while ago and had no use for them, so she sent them to their intended recipient. And now that recipient was presumably about to tear a chunk out of her for ignoring the clear signals she had sent about wishing to be left alone.

She'd suspected that this might happen. But she'd kind of hoped that it wouldn't happen when she was wearing scruffy old clothes, covered in paint and mud, with her hair a complete disaster.

"Of course, I thought you'd be talking to another person. You know, like a human being. Maybe on the telephone. But, no, you were talking to some bug."

"Bugs need friends, too," Rebecca replied. She smoothed her hair down. Arabella, as always, looked pristine.

"They do. And you're a good friend."

Rebecca blinked.

Arabella didn't seem angry. In fact, she seemed nervous if her inability to make eye contact was anything to go by.

"So are you," Rebecca whispered.

Arabella chuckled. She looked to the low garden fences that surrounded them.

"Can we talk? Inside, maybe?"

Rebecca nodded. She wiped her hands on her dirty jeans and gestured towards the open kitchen door. Arabella stepped inside. Rebecca followed her, pausing to hold onto the doorframe as she divested herself of her muddy work boots.

"Can I get you a drink?" Rebecca offered.

Arabella's perfect posture slumped.

"How can you be so nice? So... forgiving? I ran out of here, and I've avoided you for a month."

Rebecca shrugged. "Even mean people get thirsty."

Arabella snorted a laugh. She shook her head. "Thank you, but no, I'm not thirsty. I just needed to talk to you."

Rebecca held a breath. This was it. The time where Arabella

told her to back off. To most certainly not send gifts to the office.

"Okay," Rebecca said after the long pause.

"Firstly, I need to apologise for my behaviour. I shouldn't have run out of here like that. I was scared. I should have stayed and talked to you, but instead I ran. And for that I truly apologise."

Rebecca felt herself shrug again.

"It's okay," she said automatically.

"No, it's not," Arabella corrected.

"I went too far," Rebecca said. "I shouldn't have pushed you, I realise that. You were worried about me travelling because you're a good friend and I made it into... something else. I just misread some signals and, well, it won't happen again."

"Maybe you didn't misread any signals," Arabella said so softly that Rebecca wondered if she had heard correctly.

She just stared. Part of her mind was jumping for joy at the possibility of what Arabella might be admitting to. Part of her was cursing her decision to spend the whole day sweating in a muddy garden. Couldn't Arabella have an awakening on a day she felt fresher?

"Th-that..." Rebecca stammered. "I-I, well..."

Arabella chuckled softly. She stepped forward and reached up her hand. Rebecca stood as still as a statue. Arabella picked some leaves from Rebecca's hair and threw them through the open door into the garden.

"When I heard about your travel plans, I panicked," Arabella said. She continued to pick the odd leaf from Rebecca's hair as she spoke. "I had mental images of something terrible happening to you. And then I had mental images of not being with you. Not being able to see you. I didn't know what it all meant, I suspected I knew, but I didn't want to admit to anything."

She smoothed Rebecca's long hair down, adjusting it lovingly. Rebecca couldn't breathe. Arabella and her expensive perfume was right in front of her. Filling her every sense with her presence.

"I printed out Foreign Office travel warnings, and medical information about the Zika virus and about malaria. I planned to bombard you with information on why you shouldn't travel. I told myself I was being a good friend, keeping you safe." Arabella chuckled again. She ran her fingers along Rebecca's cheek.

Rebecca knew she should say something, but her mind was a complete blank. On her list of things to do that day, this was not one of them. This was something that she dreamt about. Not a reality.

"You seem to have lost the power of speech," Arabella whispered.

Rebecca slowly nodded her head.

"I don't know what I'm doing," Arabella admitted.

Rebecca knew an opening when she saw one. She leaned forward, careful to keep her clothes away from Arabella's perfectly tailored suit. She approached slowly, giving Arabella every opportunity to back away. But she didn't. Their lips softly touched. Rebecca itched to bring her hands up and hold Arabella, but she knew they were caked in mud. Again, she cursed her decision to step foot in the garden that day.

She moved her lips slowly against Arabella's, wanting to lead the way but also allowing her the opportunity to control what was happening. Pushing her too fast now would ruin everything, and Rebecca couldn't take another month like the one she'd just endured.

Slow didn't seem to be the thing on Arabella's mind. She took a fistful of Rebecca's T-shirt and pulled her closer.

"Touch me," she ordered.

Rebecca's mind crumbled at the thought.

"But I'm dirty," she pointed out, wincing at how stupid she must have sounded.

"I don't care," Arabella replied. She wrapped her arms around Rebecca, pulling her close before returning her lips to the kiss. Harder and more frantic this time.

Rebecca hesitated for a second before clasping her arms around Arabella and running her hands along the woman's back. The kiss was growing in intensity and Rebecca was getting lost in it. She wanted to get lost in it, wanted to kiss and hold Arabella for as long as she could. Worried that the moment would soon end. But if that was a possibility, she needed to know now before she got her hopes up.

She pushed Arabella away gently and took a step back.

"I need to know what this is," Rebecca said carefully. "I… I have feelings and I'm not ready to be—"

"Hurt," Arabella finished. "I know, I'm sorry. I got carried away. I'd been thinking about that all the way over here. Longer, if I'm honest with myself."

Rebecca's hands trembled at the admission.

"Don't apologise, I'm the one who kissed you," she pointed out. "But I just need to know what this is."

"I don't know," Arabella admitted. "I've never been interested in women, never even considered being with one. This is all very new to me."

"Why me?" Rebecca asked, her insecurities tumbling out.

Arabella smiled and reached up to tuck hair behind Rebecca's ear.

"You're special, unlike anyone I've ever met. And I can't stop thinking about you. Anyone would be lucky to be with you."

Rebecca felt her cheeks heat up.

"I… am going to get a bottle of water," she decided.

She turned from Arabella, walked to the opposite end of the kitchen, and opened the fridge. She was thankful for the cold air that hit her face, despite the chilly February weather outside. She quickly glugged down some water. Her mind was racing.

"I don't want to hurt you, it's the last thing I want to do," Arabella said. "And I'm only just starting to figure all of this out in my mind. It seems every time I spend a few moments with you, I completely re-evaluate my life. I was happily engaged, or so I thought. But you opened my eyes to the truth, I didn't want to marry Alastair. I didn't want to give up my work. Actually, not my work. My freedom, I didn't want to give up my life and become someone else. And, I was pretty sure I was as straight as they come but, no, apparently I'm not."

Rebecca laughed a little. "Sorry for confusing everything for you."

Arabella smiled. "I'm glad you have. I could have suddenly woken up from this fog when I was sixty and wondered what on earth I'd done with my life."

Rebecca looked at her seriously. "I haven't, like, brainwashed you, have I?"

Arabella laughed loudly. "No, I don't think so. You just woke me up."

"So, you're gay now?" Rebecca asked.

She'd heard stories about straight women suddenly deciding

they wanted to test out being a lesbian. She didn't want to be Arabella's test. She cared too much about her for that. It would break her heart when Arabella stopped having fun and went back to her real life.

"I don't think so." Arabella leaned against the kitchen counter, looking pensive. "I have feelings for you, I haven't thrown myself at any other women and I don't have an urge to."

Rebecca breathed a tiny sigh of relief.

"I can't promise you anything," Arabella admitted. "All of this is extremely new, not to mention scary, to me."

Rebecca nodded, remembering how she felt when she was figuring out her own sexuality in her teens. She couldn't imagine suddenly having her life turned upside down in her forties.

"I don't want to jump into bed," Rebecca said quickly.

Arabella's face flushed a dark red. Her eyes widened, and Rebecca had to stop herself from laughing at the shock Arabella expressed.

"Me neither!" Arabella replied. "I… I don't mean that you're not… that I… I mean…"

"It's too soon," Rebecca added helpfully.

"Yes, exactly." Arabella breathed a sigh of relief. "I'm still sorting a lot of things out."

"I bet," Rebecca agreed.

Arabella still looked a little shaken.

"Are you sure I can't get you a cup of tea? Coffee?" Rebecca offered. "I can get out of these muddy clothes and we can sit down. You can tell me all about the terrible diseases I'm going to catch on my trip."

Arabella snorted a laugh. "I don't want to interrupt your gardening, you were making friends out there."

Rebecca picked up the kettle and carried it over to the sink to fill it up. "I'll live. Stay. We can chat, if you like? I've missed you."

"I've missed you, too," Arabella confessed. "And I'd love a cup of tea."

CHAPTER 32

ARABELLA KICKED off her shoes and brought her legs up underneath her on the sofa. She looked nervously around the living room, wondering if she was doing the right thing. When she'd set off from the office, she'd only intended to thank Rebecca for the photos and to apologise for her behaviour.

Heavy traffic had given her more time to think. She decided an apology wasn't quite enough, maybe a quick explanation of her actions was also deserved. By the time she arrived in Croydon, she had decided that Rebecca deserved the truth. Or as much of the truth as Arabella had managed to figure out, anyway.

Rebecca entered the room with two steaming mugs of tea. She handed one to Arabella and then took a seat in the armchair beside the sofa.

"Freaking out?" Rebecca asked.

"A little," Arabella admitted.

She sipped the hot liquid. It was true, British people did fortify themselves with tea. She already felt a little braver. "I'm starting to realise that a lot of my life has been me doing what I think I ought to do. What other people want me to do. Rather than what *I* want to do. I'd never considered that until we drove back from Portugal."

"What did I do to make you change your mind?"

"You gave me a speech about how people in love should be a team." Arabella chuckled. "I thought you were young and naive. That you didn't understand how relationships worked. But then I thought that there must be some truth to it. You'd clearly experienced relationships like that."

Rebecca inclined her head but remained silent. She'd changed out of her gardening clothes and now wore jeans and a cosy-looking sweater. She'd taken the time to brush her hair and apply some light make-up. It made Arabella's heart beat a little faster to think that she had taken the effort for her. Not that she needed to. Rebecca was one of those natural beauties who looked great in any situation.

"The more I thought about it, the more I realised that I didn't want to be with Alastair. When you told me that I should marry someone because I loved them, it sounded like a crazy idea. And that's when I really started thinking and I realised something that shocked me."

Rebecca raised a questioning eyebrow.

"I don't know how to be happy."

Rebecca blinked. "What do you mean?"

"I mean what I said; I don't know how to be happy. I've never really sought out happiness. My parents were always very miserable and negative, so I have no problem identifying what I *don't* like. But finding something I like, seeking out something that will make me happy, I struggle with. That must sound stupid to you."

Rebecca shook her head. "No, no, I think I know what you mean. You've never really thought about being happy. You had a plan in front of you, so what was the point in seeing if it made you happy?"

"Exactly." Arabella sighed in relief that Rebecca got it.

She'd been worried that it sounded ridiculous. She sipped at her tea again, fortifying herself for the next round of admissions. "By the end of the trip home, I knew that I didn't want to be with Alastair anymore. But I didn't know what I did want. I snuck out of the party and had to seek you out. The lens cap was just an excuse."

"No! Really?" Rebecca feigned shock.

"Shut up, I'm spilling my heart here."

"Sorry." Rebecca grinned. "Please, continue."

"I felt a pull towards you, I tried to convince myself that it was friendship. That you were the first person I'd really been able to speak to. You weren't like other people I knew, you told me the truth and you told me when I was being ridiculous. I didn't feel I needed to pretend with you." Arabella leant forward and placed the mug on the coffee table. "I feel stupid," she admitted. "Spilling my soul like this."

Rebecca placed her mug alongside Arabella's and reached forward to take her hand. "You don't have to explain to me if you don't want to."

"It's not that, it's... I just feel that I don't know anything anymore. My life is being turned upside down, and I don't know which way is the right way up anymore. I had a plan, but now I don't think that's what I want. And suddenly what I want is important to me."

"But you don't know what you want?" Rebecca guessed.

"Exactly." Arabella ran her thumb over the back of Rebecca's hand.

Rebecca stood up and sat on the arm of the sofa, beside Arabella.

"Well, let's start at the top. Do you know what you don't want?"

"I don't want to marry Alastair," Arabella chuckled.

"Good. He's an idiot."

"Actually, he thinks I should be with you," Arabella admitted.

"As I said, really nice chap, great instincts," Rebecca added quickly. She removed her hand from Arabella's and wrapped an arm around her shoulder. It felt nice, comforting, supportive. Arabella leaned into it.

"What else don't you want?" Rebecca asked.

Arabella shrugged.

"I don't know. I love my job, but it doesn't excite me anymore. And I'm wondering if it's what I want or what I fell into."

"Well, you practically own the company, don't you?"

"Sort of," Arabella confirmed.

"Then take a break. I'm sure you can afford to take some time off. Take a sabbatical, or whatever posh people call it when they take a month off to find themselves. Maybe find Buddhism. Shall I find you a guru?"

Arabella shrugged Rebecca's arm off from her shoulders and jabbed her in the side playfully.

Rebecca giggled and backed away. "I'm sorry, I'm sorry!"

Arabella stopped her attack and thought for a moment. "What would I do with time off?"

Rebecca bit her lip.

"Out with it," Arabella pushed.

"Travel with me," Rebecca said. "My first stop on my grand tour is Scotland. Safe, secure Scotland. A short flight, no shots needed. I'm going to go to the cities and then ramble around the countryside a bit. If you can't decompress and sort your life in Scotland, then there's no hope for you."

Arabella laughed for a moment before looking seriously at Rebecca.

"Do you mean it?"

"You coming with me? Yes, absolutely. I mean, I'm not suggesting we sleep in the same room or anything. Just travel companions. We can see some stuff, talk, get to know each other. It will be good, for both of us. No pressure, no commitments."

Arabella furrowed her brow at the idea. Could she do it? Did she dare? Taking time off work was doable. And she'd never really seen much of Scotland. Maybe a prolonged holiday was what she needed. To breath in some fresh Scottish air. And to spend some time with the woman she couldn't seem to stop thinking about.

"It's a stupid idea. I'm pushing again, I'm sorry." Rebecca stood up to return to her seat.

Arabella reached out and grabbed her hand. "Let's do it."

Rebecca turned and stared at her with a surprised grin. "Really? Like... really? You'll come with me?"

"Yes, you set the agenda, and I'll follow you. Be my guide of the Highlands. I promise I'll even eat some haggis."

Rebecca pulled Arabella to her feet and into a bear hug. Arabella breathed in the subtle scents of Rebecca's shower gel and hairspray. She'd never realised how tantalising those smells could be. Alastair had always smelt of strong cologne that she'd never enjoyed.

Rebecca was jumping up and down with excitement. "That's amazing! I promise you it will be great, you'll love it."

Arabella jumped a little with her, allowing Rebecca's happiness to wash over her. Maybe she was still learning how to find her own happiness, but appreciating and sharing in Rebecca's was becoming second nature.

CHAPTER 33

REBECCA KNEW something was wrong the moment she walked into the airport. It was far too busy. After spending the last two weeks trying to convince Arabella that Gatwick would be better than Heathrow, they were now walking into unexpected crowds of people.

"Don't say a word," Rebecca said to her travelling companion.

"Would I?" Arabella said sweetly.

"Of course you would."

The check-in queue for their airline was enormous and didn't seem to be moving. A man at the front was arguing with the check-in assistant.

"Why do people do that? It's not their fault, they can't fix everything," Rebecca mumbled.

"Instinct," Arabella explained.

A man in a high-vis vest walked by them.

"Excuse me," Rebecca got his attention.

He turned and smiled at her questioningly. "How can I help?"

"What's going on?" she asked. "Is there a problem?"

"Yes, there's an issue with the automatic baggage systems, it's been like this for about an hour. Where are you flying?"

"Edinburgh."

He sucked in a breath through his teeth. "I think that one will be cancelled, you can rebook for tomorrow. If you hurry, you can get a room at one of the onsite hotels."

Arabella stepped forward, smiling at Rebecca as she did.

"Could you point us in the direction of the car hire desk?"

"Absolutely, just along that back wall." He pointed in the direction and then went about his business.

Rebecca looked at Arabella in surprise. "Really?"

"Why not? A long car journey sounds like fun. I'll even do some of the driving this time." Arabella tilted her wheeled luggage and started to walk towards the car hire desk.

"As long as we can stop off overnight at a creepy castle filled with demonic porcelain dolls, I'm in!" Rebecca said.

She smiled and quickly followed after her, into their next adventure.

I sincerely hope you enjoyed reading The Road Ahead.

If you did, I would greatly appreciate a short review on your favourite book website.

Reviews are crucial for any author, and even just a line or two can make a huge difference.

CALL FOR ARC REVIEWERS

Reviews are essential for authors, especially in small genres like lesbian fiction. Regardless of quality, books without reviews quickly fall down the charts and into obscurity.

That's why authors need ARC Reviewers. These are people who are willing to provide an honest review in exchange for an early, free copy of a book.

If you would like to be an ARC Reviewer for me, please click the link below:

http://tiny.cc/amandaarc

ABOUT THE AUTHOR

A.E. Radley is an entrepreneur and best-selling author living and working in England.

She describes herself as a Wife. Traveller. Tea Drinker. Biscuit Eater. Animal Lover. Master Pragmatist. Annoying Procrastinator. Theme Park Fan. Movie Buff.

When not writing or working, Radley indulges in her third passion of buying unnecessary cat accessories on a popular online store for her two ungrateful strays whom she has threatened to return for the last seven years.

Connect with A.E. Radley
www.aeradley.com

HUNTRESS

Barista. Huntress. Hijinx.

Running from the law is Amy's only choice. When the scatty barista investigates the disappearance of her favourite customer, she finds herself in the middle of a conspiracy. Armed with a dummies guide to camping and accompanied by her best friend, she rushes to escape the Huntress sent to capture her. Can Amy save the girl and clear her name, or will she be imprisoned for terrorism?

Huntress is a fun cozy mystery. Join Amy on her hilarious romp around Britain as she tries to evade the Huntress.

HUNTRESS | PREVIEW

BY A.E. RADLEY

AMY LET out a sigh and leaned back heavily on the plastic chair of the break room. She looked at the two male police officers in front of her and shook her head in despair.

"She might be dead, you know," she told them.

The older officer smirked and looked away. Probably to prevent himself from saying anything that would upset her further. Since they had arrived, both had been cocky to say the least. They had spoken down to her; mansplaining the rules on exactly when and how to declare someone as missing. The older guy had stood by the door, presumably eager to get away as soon as possible. He leaned against the wall, his thumbs hooked onto his utility belt as he left most of the conversation to his younger colleague, Officer Raj Patel.

"I think you are jumping to conclusions based on very little evidence," Raj told her in a soft tone that made Amy want to wring his neck.

"Why do I pay my taxes?" Amy asked.

"Good one, never heard that before," the older guy said with a sarcastic laugh.

Raj turned around and gave him a look. He turned back to Amy and tried to look reassuring. He obviously hadn't had a lot of practice. Amy wondered if she should suggest he request further compassion training. Or any.

"Look," Raj said, "I get that you're worried about your friend."

"She's not my friend," Amy pointed out. For the third time. "She's just a customer."

"Do you monitor all of your customers so closely?" the older officer asked, a smirk firmly planted on his face.

Amy turned to look up at him. "She comes here to the motorway services every day, every single weekday morning. She arrives at six-thirty, has breakfast, we talk, and she leaves by ten to seven. She's been doing that every day for the last ten months. Until three days ago, when she didn't show up. Those specific details about your day, you kinda remember."

"Maybe she got a new job? Or she's sick of the swill you call coffee?" He chuckled at his own joke.

"Sorry, I didn't catch your name?" Amy smiled sweetly.

"David Rowe."

"Look, Dave," she drawled his name, ignoring his wince. "I don't expect you to understand, but some people interact with other people in a cordial and sociable manner, and they make these things called friends—"

"Thank you, Miss Hewitt," Raj interrupted in an obvious attempt to keep the peace.

"And there is nothing wrong with my coffee," Amy added.

"Tell that to my tongue," David said.

"No, thanks, you're not my type." She returned his smirk with one of her own.

"Oh, I see." David pushed away from the wall, suddenly more interested in the case. "You were sweet on her."

"Sweet on her?" Amy let out a laugh. "Who even says that anymore?"

David pulled a small notebook out of his pocket and detached the pen. He looked over the top of the notepad at her as he very slowly flipped through the pages, deliberately wasting time. Amy watched him, fighting the urge to roll her eyes at his pathetic behaviour.

"So, how long had you been in a relationship with her?" David asked.

Amy glared at him. She bit the inside of her mouth to prevent the reply that was on the tip of her tongue from being let loose. After a few seconds, she took a deep breath. "I wasn't in a relationship with her."

"But you wanted to be?"

"No," Amy defended herself. "We were just friendly."

"Friendly." David nodded his head, a sarcastic smile on his lips. "So, can you tell us the full name of this friend?"

"You know I can't," Amy sighed. She folded her arms across her chest and stared at him. He was clearly trying to antagonise her, and she wasn't going to give him the satisfaction.

"Date of birth? Place of work? Home address? Telephone number?" David listed in quick succession.

Amy looked at him for a few more seconds before turning her attention to Raj. "So, you're not going to help me?"

Raj sat back in his chair and looked apologetic. "I'm sorry, there isn't a lot we can do. This is a busy motorway service station, people come and people go. This... Carla—"

"Cara," Amy corrected.

"Sorry, Cara, she may have moved away from the area. Got a new job, like Officer Rowe suggested. There's no evidence that there has been a crime committed. Just that someone changed their pattern, which isn't against the law, Miss Hewitt."

"This is ridiculous." Amy shook her head and stood up. She pushed the plastic chair back under the table and picked up her apron from the hook on the wall. She hooped the apron over her head and started to tie it around her.

"What's ridiculous is that we're not giving you a caution for wasting police time," David told her.

"You're banned," Amy told him sternly.

"What?" he looked baffled.

"Banned. You." Amy pointed her finger at him. She walked around the table and headed towards the door. "I'm not serving you coffee until you fix your attitude."

He stared at her. "You can't do that."

"I can. I just did. And you called my coffee swill, so presumably you'll be glad to not have to drink it anymore. Banned."

She opened the door and stormed into the corridor without a look back. She angrily strode through the staff-only areas of the motorway service station. She was thankful that she was away from the general public and able to have some small respite from the crowds. She needed some time alone to process what was happening. The police clearly didn't think it was an important matter, but it was. A woman was missing.

Amy knew that Cara would have told her if she wouldn't be coming back. She had even said that she would see her on Monday morning, as she always did on Fridays. Nothing about her last visit indicated in any way that it would be her last. Something must have happened to her. Women like her didn't just vanish into nowhere. Cara was beautiful in an exotic way that Amy had just read about in books. People like that didn't just disappear.

Amy sighed. She'd not wanted to give any indication that she had a crush on Cara. She knew that doing so would give the police something to laugh about, and ensure they didn't take her seriously. She hadn't been able to keep that particular piece of information to herself. She wondered how obvious her feelings were for David to have caught on so quickly.

Despite her crush, nothing had ever happened. Every morning she would anxiously await Cara's arrival. The tall Spanish woman would stroll into the services, hair and outfit perfect despite the early hour. She would approach Tom's Café in the corner of the services where Amy would be standing behind the counter, smiling and hoping her hair was behaving for once.

Cara would order breakfast. Everything was precise. Muesli on Mondays and Wednesdays, wholemeal toast on Tuesdays and Thursdays, and a chocolate croissant on Fridays. She always sat at the same table as she waited for Amy to bring the order. When Amy brought the food, Cara would invite her to sit down. They'd talk about nothing in particular, never anything personal. Amy couldn't be sure, but it always seemed like Cara was flirting with her. At least Amy hoped she was. She was certainly flirting with Cara. Or doing her best to.

Cara stayed for twenty minutes and then left, promising to see Amy the next day or wishing her a pleasant weekend. Amy would go weak at the knees as she watched the well-heeled woman walk out of the services. It was the highlight of her every morning.

Until one day she vanished without a trace. Monday had

been a grey and miserable day, and Amy had been looking forward to seeing Cara. She'd practiced her welcoming greeting a few times. She had a witty comment all lined up and ready to go. Despite seeing the woman frequently, Amy often found herself tongue-tied in the moment she actually arrived. Which was bizarre because usually Amy could talk to anyone about anything. There was something about Cara that just prevented Amy's brain from working correctly.

As she practiced her supposedly casual greeting, she'd watched the minutes trickle by. Though Cara was a stickler for timing and details, she had been late before. But never by more than a couple of minutes. By seven o'clock Amy was ready to call the police, the army, every hospital in the area.

After checking details of all road accidents within a fifty-mile radius and finding nothing that matched Cara's description, Amy told herself that maybe she was sick. After ten months of the same schedule, it had to happen eventually. The rest of her Monday shift had gone by slowly and painfully. The only bright spot was that she had convinced herself that Cara would be back on Tuesday.

Except she wasn't.

Nor on Wednesday.

At nine o'clock on Wednesday, Amy called the local police and informed them that she wanted to declare a person missing. By midday the two clowns had arrived and the ten-minute meeting had been the least productive of her life. She vowed to never bother calling the police for anything ever again.

While Raj had attempted to be polite, his main aim of simply appeasing her was thick in the air. He clearly didn't believe Cara was genuinely missing. If Amy hadn't corrected him, he'd be out looking for someone called Carla. If he even bothered to look for anyone at all.

At least Raj pretended to be interested. David hadn't even bothered, boredom coming from him in waves. And he'd insulted her coffee. Amy made a mental note to find his photograph on the local police website and print it out and stick it on the wall to inform her colleagues that he was banned.

She rounded the last corner and stopped in front of the swinging double doors that separated the staff area and the busy motorway service station. She looked through the round glass window and watched the crowds of people. Every kind of person could be found at the services, and Amy watched as they all came together in one large crowd. Nothing connecting them except the desire to rest following a long journey.

Despite the sight of over a hundred people, Amy couldn't help but think that one essential person was missing.

"Screw the police," she mumbled to herself. "I'll solve the damn case myself."

ALSO BY A.E RADLEY

BRING HOLLY HOME

She's lost everything. Can one woman bring her home?

Leading fashion magazine editor Victoria Hastings always thought that her trusted assistant quit her job and abandoned her in Paris.

A year later, she discovers that Holly Carter was injured in an accident. Brain trauma led to amnesia and Holly cannot remember anything about her life.

Guilt causes Victoria to bring Holly home and into her life to aid her in recovery. But when guilt turns into something else, what will she do?

BRING HOLLY HOME | PREVIEW

BY A.E. RADLEY

LOUISE TOOK a deep breath and quickly started to recite the schedule to her boss.

"So, as you know, the gala is tonight. The table plan is in your room for final approval as you requested. Your car arrives tomorrow at ten o'clock to take you to Charles de Gaulle. I'll be checking out of the hotel earlier to get the Guerlain samples that you requested for your sister, so I'll meet you at the airport at quarter to eleven."

Louise knew this was an exercise in futility. Her boss knew the schedule back to front, and yet she felt the urgent need to fill the awkward silence that permeated the back of the limousine. She subtly turned her wrist in her lap to look at her watch.

"Hm," Victoria murmured.

Louise looked up to see if her boss would say anything else.

Victoria continued to look over the top of her glasses at the passing Parisian scenery.

Louise debated if she should say something else. Maybe give another rundown on the first-class menu on offer on-board the flight from Paris to New York. Maybe attempt to get a tiny amount of kudos for having changed the red meat option from lamb for the entire cabin, simply because Victoria couldn't abide the smell of lamb.

Not that Victoria would ever acknowledge any of the back-breaking, soul-destroying work that Louise did on a daily basis for the impossible-to-please woman. But she lived in hope that a nugget of gratitude would work its way into Victoria's conscience.

Maybe enough to promote her from her role of assistant. Being an assistant to Victoria Hastings was certainly prestigious. Sadly, it didn't pay the therapy bills that Louise would need if she managed to survive the role.

Louise's mobile phone rang, and she answered immediately. "Yes?"

It was that awful French man from the gazette again. Blathering on about something or other and making little sense.

"Look, I've told you before, Victoria will not be doing any interviews. If you wanted to speak to her then you should have called *before* she arrived in Paris for Fashion Week. Do you have any idea how busy she is? Of course you don't."

The man continued talking hurriedly. Louise just shook her head, not even bothering to listen to what he was saying. She couldn't believe the audacity of the man. Thinking that Victoria Hastings of all people would be able to drop everything and speak to some nobody. Did he have any idea who she was?

"Absolutely not, and don't call this number again!"

Louise huffed, hung up the phone, and tossed it into her bag.

"Damn French," she mumbled under her breath.

"Problem?"

Louise looked up and realised that Victoria had turned to glance at her. Louise took pride in her appearance, checking her reflection at least every twenty minutes to ensure she was looking her best. But the second Victoria looked at her, she felt certain that she must appear a wreck.

Victoria was the kind of woman who always looked perfect. She must have had a long conversation with Mother Nature in which she put her foot down and insisted she wasn't going to age another minute. And so, forty-seven-year-old Victoria Hastings looked like a perfectly turned-out woman in her mid-thirties. Not a hair was out of place in her fashionable blonde bob. Her makeup was light but always on point, just enough to rouge her cheeks, plump her lips, and accentuate her steely green eyes. Nothing less could be expected of the editor of one of the world's leading fashion magazines.

Louise realised that she had been silent for too long. Her panic at potentially not looking her best under Victoria's frosty glare had thrown her.

"Um. No, no problem, Victoria. Just a journalist, some awful little French man. You know what journalists are like. I don't even know why I bother sending out press guidelines. He has been calling me here and Claudia back in New York every single day... I... He..." Louise swallowed nervously.

She'd said too much, she'd bothered Victoria with details that were of no interest to her.

Victoria simply stared at her in silence. Slowly, she rolled her eyes. Louise was sure that Victoria was internally questioning the incompetence she was surrounded by. She usually did. Now it was just a matter of whether Victoria would deliver a softly spoken, but scathing, remark, or if she would ignore her.

Louise held her breath while she waited for judgement to be passed.

After a few more frosty seconds, Victoria turned and looked out of the car window again. The conversation was over.

Louise released the breath she had been holding. Silently.

Paris Fashion Week was everything she'd hoped it would be. The shows, the designers, the clothes, the city. But now it was drawing to a close. Three months of doing nothing but planning Victoria's schedule had paid off. It had been a success. Not that anyone would know it from Victoria's expression.

From the moment they had landed in Paris, her boss has been quiet and detached. More so than usual. At the best of times, no one would ever accuse Victoria of being friendly or talkative. In fact, Victoria was famously known for destroying careers with a simple look.

But the last few days had been worse than usual.

Louise reminded herself that there was just one more night between her and her comfy bed back home in New York. And the next morning she would be getting to the airport bright and early and thankfully not travelling with Victoria.

The elevator doors slid open, and Victoria put on her oversized Gucci sunglasses. She walked through the lobby of the Shangri-La Hotel, her heels tapping loudly on the marble flooring.

She could sense the receptionists discreetly looking at her as she walked past them. She imagined that they were breathing a sigh of relief at her departure.

The doorman, dressed in a top hat and a knee-length, forest

green overcoat, opened the door as she approached. She breezed through and down the steps.

She let out an audible sigh at the fact that her limousine wasn't in place. She looked up with annoyance to see that the vehicle was on its way down the hotel's driveway, just passing through the wrought iron gates.

"Apologies, Ms Hastings."

She turned to see the manager of the hotel rushing down the steps. He waved his arms frantically to hurry the black limousine up. The moment it came to a stop in front of the steps, he opened the back door and gestured into the car.

"Thank you for your stay. I do hope you found everything to your liking?"

Victoria hummed half-heartedly. While the Shangri-La was slightly above average in some respects, there had been some issues. For starters, the intolerable noise of the fan in her room and the maintenance imbecile who said he couldn't even hear the noise when she had been positively deafened by it.

She passed the grovelling man and got in the back of the limo.

"We do hope to see you again next year," the man continued, holding the door open and looking at her with a pleading expression.

Victoria felt that it was very unlikely that she'd ever come back should he continue to delay her. She wanted to get to the airport and take a few private moments to call her children to see how they were doing. She travelled a lot, but she never stopped missing them.

She was about to instruct the driver to go, regardless of the position of the passenger door, when she noticed the manager looking up the driveway with a frown. She could hear some kind of commotion from behind the car.

"*Excusez-moi,* Madame Hastings!"

She glanced out of the back window. A scruffy-looking man was running towards the car. It looked like he had run through the gates as they were being closed. He held up a piece of paper and was running determinedly towards her. Two doormen and a security guard were chasing after him.

She turned around and called out to the driver in a bored tone, "Go."

The hotel manager closed the passenger door and the car slowly started to edge forward, the sharp turn of the driveway making a quicker departure impossible.

She heard shouts behind the car and rolled her eyes. It seemed nothing was going to go right during this trip.

There was a thump on the window. The scruffy man stood beside the car, holding up a Polaroid photograph. Victoria felt her mouth fall open in shock at the image.

It was Holly Carter. Her former assistant. The one who had abandoned her without a word exactly one year ago. However, there were vast differences between the Holly she had known and the woman in the photograph.

In contrast to Holly's long locks, the photograph showed a woman with short hair. Victoria's artistic sensibilities balked at the change. Long hair was finally back in fashion and the girl had chopped all of hers off. Not that Holly was ever one to toe the line when it came to fashion trends.

But the real shock was the unresponsiveness in her eyes. They no longer sparkled, there was a dullness to them that Victoria had never seen before. And Holly's already pale skin seemed paler, almost sickly in appearance. The forced smile failed to distract from the fact that she looked quite frightened.

As quickly as the photograph had been slapped onto the glass, it was pulled away. Each doorman grabbed one of the scruffy man's arms and dragged him away from the car.

"Wait," she instructed the driver.

Victoria felt the brakes being applied, and the car came to a jolting stop. She opened the door and stepped out of the car.

The man was now on the tarmac, the two burly doormen on top of him, trying to hold him down. He looked up at her.

"You know her?" he asked, his voice thick with a French accent.

"Let him go," she commanded in a soft tone.

The doormen looked in confusion at the manager who was standing helplessly by. He quickly waved his hands up to indicate that they should let him go.

Slowly, the man climbed to his feet. He clutched the photo in his hand and looked at Victoria expectantly.

She looked him up and down. She had no idea who he was or what he wanted, but he seemed to know Holly. And that was enough to grant him a few moments of her time. Even if she was running late.

She pointed to the car.

"Get in," she instructed.

ALSO BY A.E RADLEY

MERGERS & ACQUISITIONS

A crush on your boss is bad. A crush on her mortal enemy is worse.

Sophie Young is on cloud nine now that she works for her idol Kate Kennedy — owner of the best advertising agency in Europe.

When a top client requests that Kate works on a lucrative project with the notoriously fastidious Georgina Masters, Sophie knows that things are about to get tough. What she doesn't anticipate is Georgina setting her romantic sights on her.

Stuck between two fiery women and desperately trying to keep the peace, Sophie has to attempt to balance the fragile merger, keep her job, and appease both women.

Mergers & Acquisitions is a fun lesbian romance that's impossible to put down. Find out who Sophie chooses today.

BY A.E. RADLEY

CHAPTER ONE

"A sports car?" Kate repeated. She furrowed her brow at the idea.

"Yes, silver and red and really, really fast," Yannis said.

He stood up and paced excitedly around the meeting room. Yannis was tall, over six feet. His lanky frame seemed at odds with his constant need to bound around.

Kate suppressed a chuckle as she watched him pace. She appreciated his enthusiasm, no one wanted to work with a miserable client. But Yannis was almost too enthusiastic. He switched from one major project to another without stopping to catch his breath.

"Why a sports car?" Kate queried.

"We build engines, sports cars need engines. This is fantastic," he announced.

Kate suspected that Yannis felt his high-intensity enthusiasm would wear off on those around him. Bouncing around meeting rooms with excitement and informing people that things were fantastic were his way of injecting passion into a project.

Yannis was certainly a successful businessman, but he also was primarily an ideas man. Leaving the details to others. Like her.

"It's... different," Kate allowed.

"Different is good. Exciting." Yannis paused in front of the windows that overlooked the sprawling City of London. "We need to be different. We need to move, grow, change, adapt." He leaned closer to the glass and peered out of the window. "You can see my house from here."

Kate rolled her eyes good-naturedly. She stood up and walked around the meeting table to join him by the window. This wasn't the first meeting she had spent chasing after the excitable man, and it probably wouldn't be the last.

"This is east, yes?" He pointed out of the window. Before she could reply, he was staring intently into the distance, looking for landmarks.

"Yes," she replied. "Yannis, let me just get this straight in my mind. Atrom are going to build a sports car—"

"Ten," he corrected, still gazing over the city to get his bearings.

She felt her eyebrow raise. "Ten?"

"Ten," he repeated. "Selling for a million pounds. We'll only sell ten. I'm having one, of course."

Kate looked skywards. "Right, okay. Atrom are going to build ten sports cars, each priced at one million pounds, and you will buy one for yourself?"

Yannis looked at her. He smiled and nodded his head. "Yes,

that's it. And this is big news, so I need my favourite marketing guru to tell the world for me."

"And we'll be more than happy to help," Kate assured. "I assume you want the works? Press releases, websites, viral campaigns, video campaigns, news slots?"

"Everything. International," Yannis said. He looked at her seriously. "It is very important to me that this is international news."

"That's definitely something we can do." Kate mentally put together a quick marketing brief. While she considered Yannis an idiot for investing in a project that was a glorified toy for himself, she welcomed the money the project would bring.

"It's a big job," he said.

"It is," Kate agreed. Huge, in fact. Atrom Engineering was by far their biggest client, in terms of size and profitability. The introduction of a new product, and all that went with it, meant a huge amount of income for Kate's agency, Red Door.

Yannis Papadakis was the kind of CEO that Kate adored. He was rich, eccentric, and didn't think twice about spending a small fortune marketing his already successful engineering company.

"I had lunch in New York last week," Yannis continued. "With Georgina Masters, you know her?"

Kate tried to control her grimace. "I've met her a couple of times. Award ceremonies, conferences. That kind of thing."

"Mastery is considered to be the best advertising agency in America." Yannis walked back to the meeting table. He sat down and opened his MacBook. He hunched over the small machine and typed in his password. "Georgina really knows her stuff."

Kate hummed noncommittally at his mention of the

woman. If life were a cartoon, Georgina Masters would be her arch nemesis. The two women were constantly compared within the industry and by the media. They were both businesswomen in their forties, give or take, who had set up successful marketing companies in a male-dominated sector. Of course they were often compared. But comparisons are rarely kind; they certainly hadn't been between Kate and Georgina.

Kate had come to loathe the very mention of Georgina Masters. She was sure Georgina felt the same way about her.

"She is very interested in the sports car industry," Yannis was saying. He turned his MacBook around so Kate could see the screen.

She stepped away from the window and walked towards the table. She wasn't particularly interested in whatever Yannis was about to show her, but she knew she had to make an effort.

"This car was built by some guys in California, they are trying to go for the world land speed record. Georgina is representing them."

Kate picked her glasses up from the table and put them on. She peered at the website. It was garish. She had no doubt that many would think it was a fantastic example of modern web design. Flashing images, unclear navigation, lightboxes popping up. To Kate, it was gimmicky and crass. Just what she had come to expect from Mastery.

"It's a bit… flashy. Don't you think?"

Yannis grinned. "Yes," he agreed.

Kate removed her glasses and tapped the arm on her lip. "If this is the style you like, we can definitely follow this example. Maybe tweak it a little so there's not quite so much… visual noise."

Yannis spun the MacBook around to face him again and

started to type. "I want you and Georgina to work together on this. Red Door and Mastery working together. Hand in hand. Then, this project would have the best marketing minds in America and in Europe. Together, the three of us can make something really exciting."

Kate blinked. She stared at Yannis, but he was again lost in his computer screen and oblivious to her reaction.

"You want us to work together?" Kate couldn't shake the shock from her tone. "Georgina and me? Working together?"

"Yes, isn't it perfect?" He didn't look up.

"Perfect isn't quite the word I'd use," Kate confessed. The last thing she wanted was for Georgina Masters to swoop in and take all the glory. And, potentially, the entire Atrom contract. "Yannis, we've worked together for years. I like to think we have a good working relationship?"

Yannis was focused on his screen. "Yes, yes, of course."

Kate knew he was only half-listening to her. "And Atrom and Red Door have always worked well together, haven't we? We can directly attribute the twelve-percent sales growth Atrom experienced last year to Red Door's advertising campaigns. Bringing in another voice, it could be tricky."

Yannis patted the seat next to him, still focused on his screen. "Look at this."

Kate rolled her eyes and shuffled around a couple of seats at the round meeting table. She put her glasses on again. Yannis gestured to a presentation chart on the screen.

"We need to get more social," he explained to her as if she were a child.

The presentation bore the Mastery logo. Kate pursed her lips. Clearly Georgina had presented this to Yannis and convinced him to take a new direction. Upon closer examination, it was clear that Yannis had been enticed by pie charts and line graphs that showed upward trends.

Competitor agencies pitching to existing clients wasn't a new thing. Any marketing director worth their wage would use any opportunity to speak to decision-makers. Subjectivity was not just the beauty of the marketing industry; it was also its curse.

In other businesses, a job may be a simple predefined product. The business makes widgets, a widget has set parameters. The business decides its success on widgets produced.

But marketing involves so much more. Marketing can be good or bad, or good *and* bad at the same time. A logo can be loved and hated within one focus group.

The individuality of marketing allowed seeds of doubt to be planted by competitors. A magic formula could be proposed, fancy charts could be distributed and buzzwords deployed. All business owners want to recreate the success of other businesses, so a marketing agency promising such success was a potent thing.

Kate looked at the presentation with interest. As she thought, it contained all the generic statistics regarding social media success rates—the standard lure marketing agencies used to hook new prospective clients.

"Engineering firms can only benefit from social media to a point," Kate explained. It was a conversation they'd had several times before. Each time she explained it, Yannis agreed and understood. But within a few weeks, his flighty mind had forgotten and she was left to repeat herself. "The average person on the street doesn't care that the engine on a train is made by Atrom."

"We need to be a part of the conversation," Yannis insisted, clearly repeating the buzzwords he'd recently heard.

"There is no conversation about your sector, Yannis," Kate replied. She took off her glasses and let out a small sigh. Competitor interference in marketing was a common thing. One day a client would be happy, the next they would have read an article and would be explaining what they felt her agency needed to do.

Kate spent most of her days explaining to clients that she knew their market better than the competition. The difficulty was, this was Yannis. The phrase *bee in his bonnet* might have been created specifically with him in mind. Once he had an idea, nothing could make him let it go.

"Georgina has more information on this," Yannis explained. He gestured to the screen. "You understand all of this better than I do, anyway. But the thing to take away here is that this is exciting! We are going to build sports cars, and I want everyone to know about them. We can work together and make this the best campaign ever. Between us, I'm positive that we can make The Bolt something that everyone is talking about."

"The Bolt?"

"I'm thinking of calling it The Bolt." Yannis closed the MacBook and placed his fingers on top of it, protecting the secrets within. He leaned close to Kate. "I am still working out all of the details, but I can feel this is going to be a huge success." He smiled at her, willing her to join him in his excitement.

While his passion for the project radiated from him, Kate felt utterly unable to join in. She didn't want to work with Mastery. The whole point of running her own agency was that she didn't have to work with anyone.

"Yannis," Kate said carefully, "while working with Mastery

would be wonderful, I'm not sure how we can work out the logistics. They are based in New York. You and I are based in London. Trying to split the workload, coordinate the teams, that would be very difficult."

"We're a modern world," Yannis told her. "We have video conferencing, Internet, and airplanes." He stood up and started to pack his belongings into his laptop bag. "I need the best, Kate. That's you in Europe. But I need the American market. Do you know how many millionaires are in America?"

"Not off the top of my head," Kate admitted.

"Me neither, but it's a huge country, so there must be a lot. Picture it, my Bolt driving down Sunset Boulevard, maybe driven by a movie star or a pop singer. Who knows?"

Kate knew when his mind was made up. In his head, he was already winning awards and being proclaimed the genius behind the sports car of the decade. Yannis had often explained that his success was borne entirely from his sheer willpower to make success happen. He was dogged in his approach, unwavering in his beliefs. If he wanted Kate and Georgina to work together, that is exactly what he would have.

Any further argument from Kate would just make her sound awkward. As much as she hated the idea, her best course of action now was to play along.

Georgina wasn't a fool, she didn't get to where she was by not spotting an opportunity. There was no way she'd just stumbled upon Yannis. She'd sought him out, presumably armed with enough statistical information on the car industry to put Jay Leno to shame.

It was clear to Kate that Georgina was after the Atrom Engineering account. Now it was up to Kate to do everything she could to hang onto it.

Published by Heartsome Publishing
Staffordshire
United Kingdom
www.heartsomebooks.com

Also available in paperback.
ISBN: 9781912684090

First Heartsome edition: June 2018

Made in the USA
Columbia, SC
15 July 2018